Guarding Charon

International Best Selling Author
KateMarie Collins

Solstice Publishing - www.solsticepublishing.com

Guarding Charon

By

KateMarie Collins

Guarding Charon

For Jenn

Merry meet, merry part,

And merry meet again.

Guarding Charon

Chapter One
October

"Grace, come find me in my office when you're done," Mr. Jones called out as he walked through the kitchen.

Grabbing at the towel slung over her shoulder, she threw it at the counter in front of her. She grasped the edge, her stomach sinking to the soles of her feet. She knew what was coming. Bruce had been ghosting the restaurant for a month now. Sometimes outside, sitting on the hood of his car. Other times, holding court in a corner booth with his cronies. He knew where she worked now. Being fired was just a matter of time.

Tearing off her ponytail holder, she reached up to smooth back her brown hair before twisting the scrunchie around it one more time. If she was going to be fired, she'd at least look presentable.

This had become routine. She'd dated Bruce briefly, back in high school. Long enough to know he wasn't the guy for her. He never really let go, though. Four years later and he still chased after her. And every other woman in town between sixteen and thirty-five. The only difference was that Grace had said no to him.

She dusted crumbs off her apron before making the short walk to Mr. Jones' office. The door was open slightly, but she still knocked as she slid up to the framing. "Yes, Mr. Jones?" She was certain she knew what was coming.

Looking up, the balding manager refused to make eye contact with her. "Sit down, Grace. And shut the door. No one else needs to hear this."

She sidled into the room, closing the door quietly behind her. Lowering herself onto the edge of the chair in front of his metal desk, she folded her hands in her lap. And waited.

He tapped a few keys on his keyboard before facing her. Even then, he focused on a spot on the wall behind her.

"Grace, I want you to understand that I think you do a great job. Kitchen's never run better. It's just that…well, business has taken a dive over the last month."

"Since Bruce Davis started coming around."

He nodded, "Yes. The Davis family isn't one I can cross. They run the town, Grace. If Bruce has his sights set on you, he's going to get what he wants. And his family's going to help him."

"By making every single person who hires me fire me." She couldn't keep the bitterness out of her voice.

Leaning back, he sighed. "I know this isn't the first time you've heard this all, Grace." He paused, his fingers nervously tapping on the arm of his chair. "I tried to keep you on, I really wanted to give you a shot. But the bottom line is what pays my mortgage, keeps my kids fed. When Margo Davis announces at the country club that she won't be back until you're gone…people listen."

Grace rose, "I'll go get my stuff. Thanks for at least trying." She held a hand out to him. "Can I at least put you down for a reference if I ever get an interview with someone?"

He looked at her hand but didn't take it. "Sure." He turned his attention back to his computer monitor.

Grace let her hand fall and left the room, not bothering to close the door behind her. This was her life since he'd come back from college. She'd get a job, he'd find out where, she'd get fired after word got around. No one thought Bruce Davis' "fiancée" should be doing manual labor. Only Grace had no intention of ever marrying the jerk.

Silently, she untied the apron around her waist. Hanging it on a peg near the back door, she glanced around to make sure none of her coworkers were watching her leave. Not that she'd made friends here. The women all thought she was insane for not going out with Bruce. And the men all wanted to be him.

She pulled her purse and dark green jacket out of her locker, but didn't bother to put the lock back on. She wasn't coming back. She slid her arms through the sleeves before digging for her bus pass. Without a job, there was no car of her own. Or apartment.

Bruce and his posse hadn't been in the restaurant that night. Which meant he was probably out front, waiting for her. Ready with a ride home if she wanted it. Only it would be on his terms and without any care for her needs. Her dreams.

She pulled the back door open and poked her head out. The alley was dark, but clear. Just a few stray cats trying to find a meal in an open trash can. Slinging her purse across her chest, she shoved her hands into her pockets and headed for the street. If she was lucky, she'd be on the bus home before Bruce knew she wasn't inside anymore.

Her mind tried to think of a plan. Something. The only way to really get away from Bruce, from everyone and everything, was to leave town. Small towns where everyone knew your business hadn't appealed to her since she broke it off with him after their senior prom. Rumors about why circulated like wildfire across a dry wheat field. That she wanted sex and he refused her. That she was a man in drag all this time. That she was stupid. None of them knew the truth. Not even her parents.

No one knew he'd tried to rape her, beat her when she refused his demands. With his father running the police department, she knew they wouldn't believe her. No one would.

She ran, hid. Snuck back into the house while her parents slept. Hid the bruises until they healed. Told her parents she just didn't feel worthy of his love. And they believed the lie.

They graduated. He left town for college. And she moved on. Took a few classes, worked at a job she loved. And felt like she was safe at last.

Then, he graduated and came home to work with his dear old Dad. Had a badge now, and a gun. And told people the only thing missing in his life was Grace to be at his side as his wife.

The whoosh of air brakes broke through her thoughts as the bus stopped in front of her. She stepped on right after the doors opened and found a seat near the front.

Trying to forget everything, she pulled out her phone. One text, from an unknown number.

Too bad u lost another job. Can't be many left in town 4 u now.

She blocked the number. Again. Bruce would use anyone's phone to reach her. But she was tied to her parent's contract and couldn't change hers. Without a job, it was one more thing she couldn't control in her life.

Tears threatened to spill from her brown eyes. *Damn it*, she thought. *I'm trapped. Pretty soon, there won't be anyone willing to hire me. I'll have to give in, marry him. Or disappear somehow.*

Staring out the window, she didn't pay much attention to the shops or houses the bus passed. Her earbuds had died recently, and she hadn't replaced them yet. She couldn't even listen to music on her ride home.

Home. That was a laugh. More like prison, she thought. Her mom was a social climber, eager to get a larger slice of the pie. And had no understanding about why Grace didn't want to plan her "wedding" yet.

Her dad wasn't any help. He worked long hours for the post office. When he came home, he wanted peace. To relax in his chair. "Do not disturb" had been the rule since she'd been a small child.

The bus made a turn, heading down her street. At least Bruce hadn't tracked her down on the bus. Reaching up, she pulled the cord to signal for a stop. She stood, one hand grabbing the chrome bar to steady herself against the swaying motion of the bus. She nodded once to the driver in thanks as he opened the door for her to leave.

Stepping out into the cool night, she shoved her hands into her pockets. Summer wasn't quite over yet. But the slight chill told her that fall wasn't far around the corner. Not that it mattered. She was stuck no matter what season it was.

Glancing up at the house, she saw lights in the living room and nowhere else. Briefly, she thought about going around to the back door and trying to get to her room unnoticed, but she dismissed that quickly. Her mom would know she'd lost another job already. There was going to be a confrontation no matter what door she went through. She took a deep breath and strode up the path to the house. Might as well get this over with.

She opened the front door and closed it behind her. "Hey, Dad," she said as she pulled her jacket off and hung it on a too-ornate-for-the-room coat tree.

She heard him shift in his chair. "Mom told me you lost another job today. What's the matter? Too stupid to clean dishes right?"

"No, Dad. He said he loved how I ran things. Business was slow, though, so someone had to go." She crossed to the arched opening on the other side of the room. "I'm pretty tired, so heading to bed early." She headed down the hallway to her bedroom. If she moved fast enough, she could avoid her mom. She hoped.

"Gracie, baby, is that you?" Grace's heart sank as her mom's shrill voice called out from the kitchen. She stopped, her hand on the knob. So close!

June came down the hallway, busily drying her hands on a towel. "Oh, baby. Bruce called and told us how you quit another job." She reached out to hug her, and Grace knew better than to refuse. "Don't you worry, baby. You and Bruce can set a date now, you'll lose yourself in planning the wedding. You don't need to work, after all."

Twisting the handle, she looked at her mother. "Mom, there's not going to be a wedding. I'm not marrying Bruce. See?" She held up her bare left hand. "No ring." She wiggled her fingers for emphasis.

Her mom's lips tightened into a disapproving line. "That's because you're too stubborn, Gracie Lynn! That man's being very patient with you, Lord bless him. You're denying us a beautiful life!"

Grace arched her eyebrows. "'Us?' Sorry, Mother. But I'm not paying the price for you to live in luxury." She threw open the door, slamming it behind her. Turning, she put the chain on. She'd installed that about two years ago, after finding out her mom had been snooping through her journals.

Then she burned them all.

She removed her purse, tossing it on her desk before collapsing on her bed. Her hands flew to her face. Stifling the urge to scream, she tried to get rid of the headache threatening to form. She had to do something, but what? No one in town would hire her. And she didn't have enough saved up for a bus ticket to anywhere worth going. Anywhere big enough to disappear in.

Tomorrow, she'd go to the library. Search for a job with a cruise line or something. Do they still want people to teach English in Japan? Sighing, she dismissed that idea. She'd need a valid passport, for one. That cost money. And the only place local to apply was housed in the same building as the police department.

A knock at her door broke through her panicked thoughts. "Grace," her dad called. "Come out here, please. Someone wants to see you." His steps retreated.

Something in his voice gave her pause. It couldn't be Bruce. He would've said his name. And none of her friends lived in town anymore. They'd gotten out and stayed out.

She rose, glancing at herself in the mirror on the wall. Pulling out the scrunchie, she grabbed a brush and worked it through her hair quickly. That'd have to do.

Sliding the chain off the lock, she opened the door and closed it behind her. She heard her mom talking to someone, her voice nervous. Whoever this was, it wasn't someone they expected.

Grace stopped in the archway. Her parents sat on the edge of their chairs. Near the front door stood an older man, his dark suit neatly pressed. His gaze settled on her, his face lighting up. "You must be Miss Adams," he said, his voice warm. "I'm pleased to meet you. My name is Laurence Dixon," he extended his hand to her. "I'm a lawyer. Please, sit. We have much to discuss."

Grace shook his hand, surprised at the greeting. She eased into a chair nearby. "Hello, Mr. Dixon. I don't understand why a lawyer would be here to see me, though. I haven't done anything wrong."

He smiled at her. "Oh, I know you haven't, Miss Adams. I represent your great aunt, Amanda Cross."

"I don't have a great aunt, Mr. Dixon," she answered.

"She's been dead to me for decades!" Her mom stood, anger on her face. "Whatever she might want with my Gracie, she can't have it!"

Mr. Dixon looked her way. "I'm sorry, Mrs. Adams. But your daughter," he nodded toward Grace, "is named as her heir. And is of legal age to inherit. Whatever your issues with Ms. Cross may have been, it has no bearing on her last wishes."

Grace blinked. "What inheritance, Mr. Dixon?"

He turned back to Grace. "Ms. Cross has named you her sole heir, Miss Adams. She has left you her home, and entire fortune. There is but one stipulation you must fulfill to inherit."

For the first time in a very long time, Grace felt hope stirring within her. This could be her chance to escape! Disappear forever! "What's the stipulation, Mr. Dixon?"

"Ms. Cross' estate is on the Allagash River, in upstate Maine. In a small town by the name of Cavendish. Her will explicitly states that you must reside in her home for six months. The estate will pay all of your expenses for the duration. After that time, you will inherit all of Ms. Cross' assets and can dispose of the home and contents as you feel best."

"She is getting married! I'm not going to allow her to travel across the country to live in some hole in the wall!" Her mom screamed, her voice shrill.

That decided it. Grace stood, extending her hand. "Mr. Dixon, I accept the challenge. When do we leave?" She didn't care how much her mother sputtered in rage and disbelief. She was, as he pointed out, of legal age to inherit. At twenty-two, her life was hers to lead. But she had to get out from under Bruce's radar to do it. Six months in Maine? That should do it.

Mr. Dixon took her hand, placing his other one on top as they shook. "We can leave tonight, Miss Adams. I have a car outside. And a private plane at the airstrip. As soon as you're ready to go."

She smiled, genuinely happy for the first time in over a year. "Give me five minutes," she replied and then darted out of the room. It was all she could do to keep from skipping down the hall in excitement.

The door banged as she pushed it open, but she didn't care. Glancing around the room, she realized there really wasn't much she needed to take. A few personal items, sure. Maybe some clothes, a favorite sweater, her purse. It got a lot colder in Maine than Texas, she knew that much. If her expenses were to be paid, new clothes would be bought when she got there. Considering it was early October, she'd need plenty. Maybe even snow boots. *Did it snow much in Maine?* she wondered.

Her phone buzzed on the dresser. Bruce was texting her again. She reached for it, out of habit, then pulled her hand back. "All expenses," she whispered. That would include a new cell phone, with a new number.

Shoving the last few items she knew she'd need into a backpack, she left the phone and charger on the dresser.

Walking back into the living room, she saw the angry looks on her parent's faces. Her dad held a long envelope in one hand.

"You understand, correct? Not a word or there will be consequences." Mr. Dixon stood near them.

Her mother swallowed hard and nodded. Glancing at Grace, a hint of guilt played across her face. Whatever had happened, she'd ask the lawyer once they were in the air. Right now, she wanted on that plane.

"I'm ready, Mr. Dixon," she adjusted the strap of her backpack as she crossed to the coat rack. Lifting her jacket off its' perch, she waited for him with her hands folded.

He turned, his smile reaching the blue eyes. "After you, Miss Adams." He gestured to the front door. "My car is just out front."

Without another word, Grace left the place where she'd never really felt at home.

Chapter Two

Grace started down the path, her eyes searching the dimly lit street for the car. Only to stop short when she saw the limousine parked at the curb.

A hand took her by the elbow. Startled, she looked into Mr. Dixon's friendly face. "I thought you said you had a car...." Her voice trailed off.

Smiling, he gestured toward the vehicle. "Right there. I'm sorry if it startled you." He gently guided her forward again. "It's not my intention. However, Ms. Cross was insistent with her wishes. She wished that I meet you with style, treat you with courtesy, let you see what will be at your disposal for the rest of your life."

"I see," she replied. Her heart was racing. The last time she was in a limo was the night of her senior prom. When Bruce attacked her.

Mr. Dixon stopped, his face shadowed. "I should've thought it through better, Ms. Adams. I did not wish to bring up bad memories for you."

They'd reached the car. The driver came out and held the door open for her. Bright light flooded the interior. It was empty. Safe. Turning to her companion, she forced a smile on her face. "Please, call me Grace. The other is so formal." She laughed, then entered the car. Waiting until he joined her and the door closed, she asked, "What do you mean, you didn't 'wish to bring up bad memories'?"

"Your relative kept very close tabs on you. Closer than you can imagine. She knew about the young man, how he attacked you. It was one of the reasons she selected you as her heir." His face softened slightly. "Enough of that for now, however. There will be much for us to discuss once we're in the air. Your departure must be swift, lest it be noticed and someone attempt to stop it."

She watched him reach into a small cabinet and pull out some bottles of water. "Would you like one?" he asked.

She gratefully took the bottle and twisted the lid. The plastic seal broke with a series of small snapping noises. It was ice cold. Her stomach growled loudly and she realized she hadn't eaten since breakfast. Embarrassed, she looked out the window.

"There's a marvelous chef on the plane, miss. You'll be able to eat your fill."

Laughing, she asked, "How big is this plane?"

He crossed his legs, hands folded neatly on his lap. "Not large, by private plane standards. My employer had standards, but they weren't opulent or showy. You'll have an area to sleep during the flight, should you choose. And a chef was retained, as per her wishes. She wasn't sure what your favorite foods were, so there will be a variety to choose from on this trip."

"I have to admit, I don't recall her name being brought up at all. I never even knew she existed."

"That doesn't surprise me, given what she shared with me about your upbringing. Again, those answers will wait for when we're aboard the plane." He gestured toward a speaker in the corner of the back window. A small red light blinked steadily. They were being recorded in some way.

Nodding her understanding, she sipped more of her water. It was a local company, a rental. Which meant it was possible that Bruce or any number of his cronies installed the device to get dirt on the people renting the vehicle.

The airstrip wasn't far out of town. She remained silent for the rest of the short drive. Her mind, full of questions, struggled to make sense of what little she knew. Which wasn't much. A relative in Maine that she'd never heard of left her everything. The timing was perfect. She'd be able to escape Louden, be out of Bruce's influence. But who was this great aunt? And why was her mother so filled with hate for her? When the lawyer made it known they were being recorded, though, the questions stayed in her mind. She was being given the chance she needed. She wouldn't risk a slip up now. She was so close to being free!

The car slid up to a sleek aircraft, the lights blinking in the night. A woman stood waiting at the bottom of a small flight of stairs leading into the body of the plane. The limo stopped a few feet from her. "We're here," Mr. Dixon announced with a sigh. Was he worried someone would stop them?

She slung the purse across her, then grabbed at her backpack and jacket as she exited the car.

"Miss, this way please." The woman began to climb the steps and disappeared into the aircraft.

Mr. Dixon stood to one side. "After you," he said, ushering her into the aircraft.

Grace climbed the stairs. For some reason, it became very real to her. She was leaving. She stopped halfway up, suddenly afraid that Bruce had set this all up. He was waiting for her, inside.

"Miss Adams, he's not here. This is not a set-up. But we must take off before he can possibly learn you've left." Mr. Dixon spoke in hushed tones.

She let out a long breath, releasing the fear. Nodding, she all but sprinted up the last few steps and into the plane.

The interior was beautiful. Warm wood complimented with cream leather seats. A loud bang sounded behind her. Turning quickly, she saw the woman securing the door before smiling at her. "Please, find a seat and make yourself comfortable. We have our clearance already and will be taking off momentarily." She disappeared behind a thick blue curtain.

Mr. Dixon settled into a chair next to a small table and buckled the attached belt. "Ms. Cole is an accomplished pilot, but I've never been able to fully relax on take-offs or landings."

The engines roared to life and the plane moved forward. Grace dropped her bag and jacket on the floor, then moved to another seat and strapped herself in. She'd never flown before, so she had no idea what to expect.

The force propelled her back in her seat as the small plane left the ground. She dared a glance out a window and saw the lights of Louden, Texas fade away below her.

After a few minutes, the craft leveled off. Mr. Dixon unbuckled and rose. "Would you like a quick tour, Grace? Something to eat? Or shall we get straight to your questions?"

Before she could answer, a man emerged from behind the black curtain that hid the galley. Dressed in white, his short, dark hair stood out. He clapped his hands together, his head swiveling between Grace and Mr. Dixon. "Is this her? Our new mistress?" A slight accent tainted his words, but she couldn't place it.

The lawyer smiled and lowered his head for a moment. Waving his hand toward the new arrival, he made the introductions. "Ms. Adams, this is Hugo. He's going to make sure you're well fed."

She went to unbuckle and rise as the man crossed to her. She was barely on her feet before he was hugging her, then kissing each of her cheeks. "Senorita, it is an honor. How may I tempt you tonight?"

Grace hesitated, "I'm not...I don't know..."

Hugo smiled, "If you are willing to answer five questions, I can make you a meal you'll dream of!"

"Okay...what are the questions?"

"First, beef, chicken, or fish?"

She bit her lip, thinking. "Beef."

He nodded. "Next, vegetables, pasta, or rice?"

"Vegetables." She didn't have to hesitate on that one.

"Lots of pink, a little pink, or no pink?"

"Lots of pink." She laughed.

"Excellent! Just two more! Mild, medium, or hot?"

"Medium. I may be from Texas, but I don't like a really hot pepper."

He put his index fingers together, touching them thoughtfully to the tip of his chin. "Last question, and the most important. Chocolate or vanilla?"

"Chocolate!"

He rubbed his hands together quickly. "Ignore any words you may hear from my kitchen, Senorita. What comes out will be worthy of any noble house in Catalonia!" He disappeared back behind the curtain.

Grace looked at Mr. Dixon, her mouth open in surprise.

"It looks like Hugo decided you needed to eat first." He laughed. "If you'd like, we can sit and talk while he cooks."

She settled back into her chair. "I couldn't place his accent. Where's he from?"

"Catalonia. It's a province of Spain, moving toward autonomy. Barcelona is the largest city. But he's traveled extensively to learn his craft. He was retained by Ms. Cross almost twenty years ago."

"Will he be living at the house with me?"

Mr. Dixon opened a small cabinet and pulled out two bottles of water. "No, not at all. He runs a small restaurant in town. You can go there for meals as often as you like, and he'll come out to the house to cater if you're entertaining. He loves to travel and insisted on joining me on this trip. He was very excited to meet you." He handed one of the bottles to her before settling into a chair.

"Mr. Dixon, is this a safe place to talk? After what happened with the limo…" her voice trailed off.

"Very secure and safe, I assure you. No one would've been allowed to come close enough to the plane to put any sort of devices on the exterior, let alone gain access to the inside. Bruce will not be listening in." He smiled. "If you like, you can call me Larry. Mr. Dixon is extremely formal. 'Stuffy' is what your great aunt called it. We will be working closely for the next several months, getting the estate transferred to you. There is no reason to be formal when we're alone."

He leaned back, his face taking on a more serious appearance. "Grace, this is a hard thing to ask right now, but it must be discussed. You have the chance now to reinvent yourself, disappear in some ways. Amanda knows what Bruce tried to do, and how he was forcing you into a corner so you'd have to marry him. She was making plans to bring you to her home herself, when she passed away. If you want, everything is in place for me to create a new identity for you. A new name, new social security number, new driver's license. We can get the paperwork started now, have it all in place by the time we arrive in Cavendish. I only need your permission, and a name you'd like to be known by."

She stared at the bottle in her hand. To truly disappear, become someone else, would guarantee Bruce would never find her again. Even if she didn't stay in Maine after her six months were up, he would never find her.

"What about my parents?" Her voice was hushed.

"They accepted a check. Enough to guarantee your father can retire; their debts are paid in full if they choose to do that. But the money is conditional that they tell no one where you went. They know it is likely they'll never see you again, and traded the money for contact with you."

Grace slouched in her chair. Her entire body shook. They abandoned her, cut her out of their lives forever, for money. She knew she should be shocked, upset. But she felt numb. "I think I need a drink," she whispered.

She kept staring at the bottle of water in her hands, fascinated by the motion of the water as the tremors continued. Distantly, she heard ice hitting the bottom of a glass, followed by liquid being poured. It appeared on the edge of the table.

Shaking, she put the water on the table and grabbed at the glass. Amber liquid swirled around a giant ball of ice. Before she could stop herself, she downed the scotch. It burned as it traveled down her throat, numbing her stomach to match her emotions.

If they were ready to be done with her, then she would be done with them. "Let's do it."

"Very well. What would you like your new name to be?"

She stared at the glass in her hands. "Did she have any family with her last name?"

"No. She was the last Cross. Her sisters took the names of their husbands, and she had no brothers."

"That's it, then. I'll be Amber Cross." She raised her glass. "Here's to new beginnings."

He raised his as well, "To new beginnings, Amber Cross."

Swallowing some more of the alcohol, she began to try and adjust to the new name. "So, this house. What's it like? And why'd she choose me?"

Larry rose, opening an overhead compartment and pulling down a briefcase. He sat it down and spoke as his fingers worked the combination lock. "Amanda is the best one to answer those questions."

"How can she? You told me she was dead."

The locks snapped open. Raising the black leather lid, he pulled out a thick envelope and handed it to her. "I don't know what it says. But she made me promise to give this to you before I answered any questions on the house or why you."

She put the glass on the table and took the light brown envelope. The paper was heavy, rigid. Turning it over, she ran her fingers over the seal adorning the back. Embedded in the deep blue wax was a circle with a five pointed star. The initial, 'C', rested in the center.

For all the risks she'd taken in the last hour, opening this envelope seemed to have the highest stakes. A feeling overtook her, a cross between excitement and things finally becoming right in her world. She'd never given much attention to astrology or those who said a path was laid out for each person to walk. Not before now. In this instant, though, she realized her feet were firmly planted in the right direction.

Stop being melodramatic, Amber, she thought. And blinked. Her new name fit so well, as if that's what she'd always had. Grace Lynn Adams was truly gone. Time for Amber Cross to find out where her path would lead her.

Her finger slid between folds of the envelope, slowly lifting the flap free of the wax. A letter rested inside. The paper was the same high quality as the envelope. Pulling it out, she unfolded it and began to read.

My Dear Niece,

I won't address you by name. By now, I hope you've changed it from the moniker your parents gave you in preparation of the new life I've offered you. Whatever you've chosen to call yourself, you will know if it's a true name or not.

I know you're full of questions. Why did I leave everything to a relative I've never met? Why didn't your mother ever mention me? Why am I requiring you to live in Maine during the winter?

I left everything to you because I've been directed to do so. By someone I trust with my very soul. You will meet him soon enough. Never even try to lie to him, for he will know it before you utter the words.

As to the distance between the rest of the family and myself. I was a follower of the Wiccan faith, and lived my life in accordance to the Rede that guides all that believe. The rest of the family, convinced I was possessed by the devil, ostracized me. I believe that you have some of the same capacity for magic that I did. If I am right, my home will welcome you. Make you happier than you can ever imagine. And you will never wish to leave. If I'm wrong, and it wouldn't be the first time, then do what you must when the six months are over and live a life you will be happy with.

Larry will care for your needs, make sure bills are paid. The home has no mortgage, it has been owned outright for centuries now. And passed down to one that is worthy when the current occupant's time on this plane is done.

I learned too late about what Bruce did to you to help you leave when you finished high school. When I found out his scheming was getting you fired from jobs, preventing you from growing into your own person, I began to take steps to come retrieve you myself. Alas, my heart had other ideas. I can only pray to the Goddess that Larry finds you and gives you this letter before your mother marries you off to such a monster.

Come to the River House. Stay with my old friends, discover their secrets, and make them your friends. The world is yours now. Without fear.

> *Blessed Be,*
> *Amanda Cross*

Amber folded the letter again. Before she could speak, Hugo came out with a steaming plate of food. Her mind reeled from the information in the letter. Growing up in a conservative small town, she went to a Christian church. Anything else was the work of the devil. She'd gone because it wasn't something she dared rebel against. *I've already left that life, changed my name. What harm could be in being open-minded about her faith?*

She was lost in thought when the first bite reached her mouth. Flavors exploded, making her eyes go wide with surprise. "Hugo, this is amazing! I've never tasted anything like it!"

The chef beamed and bowed, "A pleasure, Senorita!" He bowed once again then left the cabin area.

Before she knew it, the dish before her was empty. She scraped her fork across the china, desperate to get every last morsel.

"Amber, there's one more thing."

She looked up, her fork still in her mouth. Larry was holding out a small box.

"This was one of Amanda's greatest treasures. She does not expect you to wear it immediately. Indeed, you may never wish to wear it at all. But she insisted you were given it after you read her letter."

Slowly, she lowered the fork on the plate. Wiping the corners of her mouth with a cloth napkin, she took the box from Larry. Pulling off the lid, she found a silver necklace on a chain. The design was the same as on the wax seal. In awe, she traced a finger around the edges of the star. The piece called to her, stirred something within her soul.

She put the lid back on, unsure what to make of the emotion it evoked. "Larry, it's been a long day. I think I need to sleep. Is there a couch on this plane?" Her voice sounded weary, even to her ears.

He nodded. Moving the short distance to the rear of the plane, he opened a door. "This should do," he stated.

Rising, she looked past him. A bed stood in the space. Grabbing her backpack and other items, she moved into the room. The pack slid to the floor as she placed the box with the pentacle on the small nightstand. Lying on the bed, she was asleep before she finished pulling the covers up to her chin.

Chapter Three

A light rapping on wood penetrated the dreamless sleep she was enjoying. "Amber, are you awake?"

Groaning, she rolled over. Whoever this "Amber" was, she needed to get them to stop. The bed was the most comfortable thing she'd ever slept in. It seemed to embrace her, no matter how she rolled. Not a single lump or dip, just soft and welcoming.

"Amber?"

"Go away. There's no Amber here. I'm still sleeping," she growled. Grabbing a pillow, she threw it over her head in hopes to drown out the person trying to rouse her.

"Amber, you need to get up. We've landed. Hugo's waiting on you to serve breakfast."

Her mind woke up, memories of everything that'd happened the night before rising about her foggy brain. *She* was Amber now. She pushed herself up on her elbows, remembering the wonderful meal she'd been served the night before. "Give me five minutes," she called out. Throwing the covers off of her, she grabbed at her backpack. It didn't take her long to change into something clean or pull a brush through her hair.

As she walked out of the room, she glanced out the windows. They were inside a building. "Where are we?" she asked.

"Bangor, Maine," Larry replied, offering her a steaming cup of coffee. "There's cream and sugar if you want some."

Nodding, she went to the table he gestured to and added some of each to the mug, stirred. "What time is it?"

"About ten in the morning. Hugo will be right out with breakfast, then we can head to the hotel. There's a lot we need to do today while we're in the city. Tomorrow, we'll make the drive out to Cavendish and your new home."

"Is it a long drive?" she asked. The words he used, "your new home," excited her. The closer it was, the more she wanted to see it. Meet the friends Amanda spoke of in her letter.

"Just over four hours, but this is the closest major airport. The hangar we're in is yours as well. It's the perfect place to keep the plane when it's not in use."

Amber sat in a chair, tucking one leg underneath her. She hadn't bothered to put on socks or shoes. The plush carpet beneath her foot felt wonderful.

Sipping her coffee, she asked, "When did we get here? I don't remember landing."

Larry sank into another chair. "We landed some time ago, about three a.m. local time. Ms. Cole executed a smooth descent. It didn't even wake me up, and I'm a light sleeper. Given everything that you had sprung on you last night, I thought it best to let you get a full night's sleep. We have enough to do today to fill it."

Hugo came out, his normal smile lighting up the room. A plate of strawberry crepes with whipped cream was placed in front of her. "Enjoy!" he exclaimed, clapping his hands together once again before disappearing.

Amber took one look at the meal and realized how ravenous she was. Picking up her fork, she asked, "What are we doing today? Why wait to head out to the house?" before diving into her breakfast.

"Several things, actually," Larry replied as he started on his own plate. "I've got a few things to wrap up in regards to your new identity. Paperwork that must be notarized, filed, for that and for you to inherit the estate. I've arranged for a personal shopper to bring some clothing choices to the hotel. You'll be able to try things on, make selections, without fighting a crowded mall."

"I don't mind the mall," she replied.

"It's not about that, actually. It's going to be better if you're not seen in public until we get to Cavendish. I have no doubt that your ex has gotten information on the aircraft. We did take a detour over Kentucky due to weather, but the flight plan will still give our final destination. We landed at night, and Ms. Cole's going to take off again once we're safely on our way to the hotel. As far as Bruce will be concerned, we landed, took on fuel, restocked the plane, and left again. This time, toward Ireland. As long as you're not seen on security cameras or photographed by a tourist, your trail will go cold."

Nodding, she ate a few more bites. "That makes sense, I suppose. Do you really think he's going to come after me already? You said my parents promised to not tell anyone where we went."

"Given what Amanda heard of him through her friends, I have no doubt he's trying to find out. You're the one who dared to tell him no. For that alone, he'll hunt you down. Once we finish up this part of the ruse, he'll be lost. If and when he figures out you never went to Ireland, you'll be so established as Amber Cross that he'll never connect her to Grace Adams." He smiled at her. "You did a good thing, leaving your cell at home. That and social media will be what he'd try first."

"I don't have anyone I'd want to call anymore anyway. And he always found ways to contact me on it, no matter how often I blocked the numbers."

"Amanda has a land line at the house, but I also set you up on this one." He tossed a phone over to her.

Catching it, she smiled. It was a new smartphone, the kind she'd wanted for a while. "You'll have to set up the passcode. Right now, it's nothing beyond a basic 0000. But this number is unlisted. It's set up where the outgoing calls are allowed, but incoming ones are restricted to numbers you approve. I hope you don't mind, but I took the liberty of adding mine as approved."

She drew the leg out from under her and pulled her knee up to her chin. Wrapping an arm around the leg, she began to play with the screen. "No, that's fine. I'm sure I'll need to talk with you off and on."

"My recommendation is to not give out your number, but take theirs. If your instincts tell you to trust them after a few meetings, then make your phone available to take their call. Otherwise, it won't ring. The call will go straight to your voicemail. This should also cut down on telemarketers."

They finished breakfast in silence. Amber concentrated on her new phone, setting a new passcode and figuring out how to work the various features and apps.

Briefly, she looked up as Hugo came in and removed her breakfast tray. "Thank you, Hugo. It was delicious," she told him with a smile before turning her attention back to her phone.

"Amber, we have to leave. Now." The urgency in Larry's voice broke her concentration. Looking up, she saw a concerned look on his face.

Unfolding herself from her seat, she asked, "What's wrong?"

"Get your things. I'll explain in the car."

Quickly, she dashed into the back of the plane. Something was wrong. Had Bruce found her? Panic rose in her as she threw her dirty clothes into her pack. The box with the pentacle went in last. She pulled the drawstring tight as she shoved her feet into her shoes. Throwing on her jacket, she slung both pack and purse over her shoulders. Darting back out, she announced, "I'm ready."

Larry looked at her purse. "Amber, leave all of your old identification here. Anything with your name on it. Social security card, driver's license, library card. All of it.

Grace Adams will be dead soon, but we need to make sure people think it was you."

She swallowed, dread filling her heart, as she pulled her wallet out of her purse. She removed the little bit of cash she had, then put it back in. Handing over the entire bag, she said, "Here. Nothing in there I want any more anyway. And I've carried that purse and wallet since high school."

Larry took it, deliberately tossing it into a corner. "What about the backpack?"

She shrugged it off her shoulder. "Same with it, yeah. I think I got it in middle school, to be honest." She set it on the table and opened it up, pulling out the box and letter from the night before. "These are the only things that wouldn't be mine."

"Okay, good. Leave it, too. Before we leave tomorrow, you'll have a whole new wardrobe anyway. And name." Ms. Cole moved the mechanism to the door and it began to lower stairs to the ground. "After you," Larry motioned to the exit.

Grasping the box and letter, Amber shoved her phone into her pocket and descended the stairs.

A black SUV, with tinted windows, sat off to the side. She waited for Larry to descend. Hugo came out first, heading to a smaller car with a large bag. Larry stood at the top, one hand on the rail, talking with Ms. Cole. She nodded in understanding, then reached to the handle that would raise the stairs again. As soon as Larry's feet touched the ground, she began to raise the stairs.

"The black one's for us," he said. "Should be unlocked."

Quickly, she moved over to the passenger side and opened the door. The interior was opulent by her standards. Leather seats, in-dash display, and more controls than she'd seen in a car before. She shut the door and began to buckle herself in as Larry slid behind the wheel and did the same.

"Larry, what's happened?" she asked, as he turned the key and the engine roared to life.

"Bruce used his contacts, put out a missing person's alert for you. Claimed you were kidnapped by 'persons unknown' but that your life was in danger. The national media's picked up on it." He put the car into gear and drove toward a ramp at the far end of the hangar. Guiding the car, he descended into a short tunnel. The wall in front of them opened, and they continued forward. "Ms. Cole is taking off now, heading to Ireland. On her way, she'll parachute out and let the plane crash into the Atlantic. By the time they realize the plane's off radar and do a search, there won't be anything but wreckage to recover. Like your purse and backpack."

"What about Ms. Cole?" Amber asked, her eyes wide.

"Don't worry about her," Larry laughed. "She used to be in the military. She's well trained in skydiving and survival. I wouldn't be surprised if you saw her in Cavendish before the week is out."

The dark tunnel began to lighten, and she saw an opening leading to a city street. Larry merged the vehicle into traffic. "Our hotel's not far. And they know how to keep an arrival secret."

She ran a hand through her hair. "Do you think they have a stylist? I know you said someone was bringing clothes for me to pick from, but I might need a haircut. Bruce never saw me with short hair. It might help."

He glanced over, nodding. "That's an excellent idea. I'll ask the concierge once we're checked in."

Amber lost herself in the view of the city around her. She'd never traveled far from home, so the high rises were a new sight. Though there were just as many smaller buildings, full of architectural details that told her they'd been there for a lot longer than the rest.

"What's over there?" she asked, pointing to an area full of ships off to the distance.

"That's the U.S. Navy base. Don't be surprised if you see a lot of people in uniform at the hotel. The Navy's got a big presence in the city." He turned left into an alley.

The car stopped outside a garage door. He honked the horn once, and the door began to rise. Driving into the garage, he pressed the brakes slowly and brought the car to a stop as the door lowered behind them.

Two men came forward and opened the car doors. "Welcome back, Mr. Dixon. Everything has been arranged as you requested." A woman, dressed in a black suit, spoke from a doorway. "If you and your companion will follow me, I'll take you up to your suite."

Amber saw Larry hand off the keys to the SUV to one of the attendants. He waved her to move around the car and accompany him to where the woman stood waiting.

Shaking her hand, he said, "Thank you, Evelyn. Ms. Cross is hoping you have a stylist available. She's interested in a new look."

The woman smiled pleasantly at Amber. "Of course. I'll find someone and send them to your suite as soon as they arrive. The shopper from Anastasia's is here already, waiting on your arrival." She opened a door and held it for them to enter a small room with closed doors for an elevator. Inserting a key into the case near the door, she continued, "I took the liberty of ordering some suitcases so it would be easier for you to take the clothing with you. Along with an assortment of personal items that Ms. Cross might need." The doors slid open and they went inside.

Amber watched as Evelyn used her key once again, this time pressing the button for the eighteenth floor as she did. "Thank you," she murmured. She hadn't even thought about replacing more than clothes, but it was going to be necessary now that all of her belongings would be lost in the crash that would fake her death.

She grasped the box and letter in her hand even tighter. Taking a deep breath, she calmed the nerves threatening to overtake her. So much had changed, so much had happened, in less than a day. For the first time, she began to wonder what she'd gotten herself into. Yes, she was going to be free of Bruce. But would she pay for that later? And, if so, what was it going to cost her?

The elevator stopped and the door slid open. A room, one wall all windows, spread out before her. "Let me know if you need anything else, Mr. Dixon. I'll send the stylist up once they arrive."

Amber barely heard the woman leave. Stepping down into the living area, she marveled at the furnishings. A fire burned in a hearth built in the center of the room. The windows looked out across the city. To her amazement, small white flakes began to fall past the window. It was snowing.

"Amber, meet Elise. She's from Anastasia's, one of the best boutiques in Bangor."

Amber turned around to meet the woman. Tall and slender, she wasn't much older than Amber. Elise shared her tastes—that much was clear. The jeans, sweater, and boots the woman wore made Amber breathless. Comfortable, chic, and classic. This was the type of look she'd always wanted to pull off, but never had the money to achieve. Her excitement over a new wardrobe went up a few notches. Whatever Elise had brought with her, she knew she'd love.

Elise smiled, "Hi, Amber! I put the clothes in your room. Shall we get started?"

Over the next two hours, she did more shopping than she'd done in three years. With Elise's help, she went through the collection the woman had brought, as well as the store's website. It took another fifteen minutes for her to complete her wardrobe.

Smiling, Elise stood up. "It's been great to meet you, Amber! Go ahead and keep everything that fit and you liked that I brought with me. The rest will be sent over from our store before five p.m. tonight." The woman consolidated the racks of clothes to make up for Amber's selections, then covered everything that would travel back with her.

Amber nodded, following her out of the room and to the elevator. "It was fun. I've never had a personal shopper before." She laughed.

Elise waved again as she maneuvered the racks into the elevator. "Be sure to ask for me if you ever want to do this again," she said as the doors slid shut.

Larry sat on the couch, flipping through some pages in a file. "All done?" he asked.

Amber flopped into a chair across from him. "Yes. I think I over-shopped, but Elise said I'd need a lot of warm gear for the winter."

He smiled. "Oh, probably. We tend to measure snow in feet in Cavendish each year." He pulled aside a piece of paper and added it to another pile. "You and I have to get some legal things done." He gestured toward the smaller stack.

She scooted forward and picked up the pile. "What's all this?"

"Some of it is to establish Amber Cross as a person. The other pile is to transfer Amanda's assets to your new name. Grab something to eat. There's a stocked kitchen over there." He pointed to the alcove near the elevator. "This is going to take some time."

Over the next several hours, Amber had her new life explained to her. The inheritance, beyond the house in Cavendish, included several bank and investment accounts. Her total net worth was now well over $50 million dollars, an amount that boggled her mind.

As she went through another sheaf of paper, the phone rang. She stopped, listening to Larry as he answered it. "That's fine. Yes, please. Send him right up," he said, then hung up the phone.

"Who was that?" she asked.

"Evelyn, the concierge. Your stylist has arrived. She's sending him up now." He scanned a few more pages in front of him. "We should be able to finish this up before they arrive."

Before the elevator chimed the arrival of the stylist, she had a new driver's license, passport, and social security card in her new name. Credit cards were ordered, and all of the legal papers were signed.

The stylist, a gentleman in his thirties, spoke softly. His one question was what she wanted. "I want it short," she said. "I don't want to color it or anything. I just need something drastically different."

Hearing the clipping of the shears made her nervous, but it was her idea to start with. She was becoming someone new. Someone Bruce or her parents would never recognize. With every snip, more of Grace Adams disappeared and Amber Cross came to life.

Chapter Four

*A*mber stretched, waking up slowly. The night before had been quiet. She ate dinner in the suite with Larry, watching the snow fall outside the hotel. After a relaxing bath, she'd spent some time packing her suitcases with her new wardrobe. Larry'd told her it was a good four- hour drive to Cavendish, to her new home, and they both wanted to make an early start of it today.

Her home. Her *home*. For some reason, the idea of having a place associated with that word excited her. She knew she'd be counting the hours during the drive, straining to catch her first glimpse of what Amanda called "The River House" as they arrived in town. Anxious to get moving, she jumped out of bed. She didn't rush getting dressed. The quality of the fabrics made her pause along the way. Heavy denim jeans, a sweater that hugged every curve. Soft leather boots that reached her knees in the same gray as the sweater. She darted into her bathroom, and stopped. Her short hair still new enough to give her pause. Did she really know the beautiful woman staring back at her? Nodding, she smiled at her image. She really was Amber now. And Amber could live without being afraid of her own shadow.

Quickly, she gathered up the make-up Evelyn provided for her. Stuffing her pajamas and the cosmetics into one suitcase, she did a sweep of the room to make sure nothing was left behind. The night before, she'd packed almost all of her new wardrobe and put it by the elevator, leaving only a small suitcase and what she'd need this morning in the room. Sure enough, she'd almost forgotten the new leather purse and wallet. Resting on the dresser next to her new cell phone on its' charger. Laughing at herself, she unplugged the phone, slipped the charger into the purse, and zipped it closed. Slinging it over her shoulder, she raised the handle on the suitcase and wheeled it out of the room.

She put it next to the others and the stack of shoeboxes next to the elevator doors. "All ready," she called out.

Larry came out of his room, a small suitcase in one hand and his briefcase in the other. "Let me grab a cup of coffee first," he said as he put his items near the door.

She jumped up on the counter as he plugged in the coffeemaker. "I don't mean to be pushy, it's just that…" her voice trailed off. Would he understand the driving need she felt to finally be someplace she could call home?

"You want to go home. I understand." He smiled as her jaw dropped in amazement. "You forget, I'm well aware of Amanda's religious views and practices. More than once, she'd come to my office or call me, tell me to buy or sell a certain stock. Help one family or ignore someone begging for charity. She embraced her Wiccan nature and lived her life by trusting her intuition. It rarely failed her."

"I suppose I can order some books about that part of her life when I get settled. I'd like to understand it better. Where I grew up, that was considered devil worship. I'm pretty sure it wasn't, though."

He finished pouring water into the machine and turned it on. The aroma of coffee slowly filled the air. "Amanda had an extensive library, so now you do as well. I'm sure you'll find out everything you might want to know about the faith from the books she had."

Nodding, she replied, "Good point. It's not like I have to find a job or anything." She laughed.

"No, not like most people do. But it is October. Amanda was well-known for her celebration of Halloween in town. Her yard and the outside of the house were often decorated, and she'd dress up to greet trick-or-treaters. It was the one time of the year where she'd do the whole stereotypical witch get up."

Amber did some quick math. "That's only about three weeks away," she said. "I guess I will have to get to work." Laughing, she gladly took the mug of steaming coffee he offered her. He'd even added the milk and sugar for her. "I suppose the first order of business will be to unpack, then find where she stored all those decorations. And hit the grocery store to make sure I'm well stocked on candy."

The conversation turned to what was available in Cavendish as far as shopping was concerned. Larry had told her the night before, as they went through all the paperwork, that there was Wi-Fi and satellite TV at the house. Amanda had left a laptop and desktop, both purchased within the last few months, so she wouldn't be totally isolated. The town itself had some great shopping, but some things would be better off being ordered online.

It didn't take them long to finish the coffee. Draining her cup, she placed it in the sink. "I feel like I should wash those," she said.

"Don't worry about it," Larry said, shrugging on a heavy wool coat. "The hotel staff goes over the room extensively after every stay."

Amber picked up the leather coat she'd purchased the day before and slid her arms into it. The aroma made her smile. She was going to have fun getting used to having access to things like this.

The elevator doors opened up, and two bellhops emerged. One pushed a cart for their luggage. Piling the suitcases and boxes on, they all squeezed back into the elevator for the ride down to the garage.

Larry's SUV was waiting for them. "Go ahead and get in," he told her as he went around to the back and supervised the loading. Without hesitation, she slid into the passenger seat and waited. Within minutes, the garage door rose and they were on the road to Cavendish.

They didn't talk much during the drive. At this point, she wasn't sure what she still had to ask. So many questions couldn't be asked yet, shouldn't be asked yet. Her instincts told her some would be answered by the house itself. How, she had no idea. But that's what her gut told her.

Maybe I'm really a witch, like Amanda was, she thought. *Larry said she went by instinct a lot. And her letter told me she thought I had some affinity for the faith. I guess I'll have to do some real research in her library.*

The scenery shifted. The city was left behind them as the terrain became more rural. Forests, rivers, fields became more picturesque, houses and small towns fewer and farther between.

The radio signal never wavered as they drove. "The reception's pretty good up here," she commented. "Back in Texas, the signal dropped before you got sixty miles from the station."

"It's satellite," Larry replied. "About the only way to go out in Cavendish. We've had a local station or two, sure. But most people shell out the monthly subscription fee. The drive into a major city is too long. Some people have older cars, limited to CD players. Now, though, the few car lots all sell them with MP3/USB plug ins or satellite subscription services. Makes it easier if you want something to listen to on the drive."

"You make Cavendish sound smaller than Louden," she couldn't keep the fear out of her voice. Trading one small town for another, one where she would be isolated due to weather for half the year, wasn't exciting. Even if Bruce was out of the picture for good. The idea of having a handful of neighbors nosing into her business was unappealing.

"It's not that small. We have around 5,500 residents. We have our own hospital, with a top-notch trauma team. The area's great for recreation and outdoor sports. Kayaking and rafting down the river during the summer, cross country skiing and snowmobiling in the winter. Plus hiking, fishing, hunting. The year round folks, the ones that live there, they're not nosy. Oh, sure, one or two will ask a question or three. But most know that Amanda passed away and I was off to bring back her heir. At most, you'll get some friendly invites to join a club or two. Asked if you want to bake cookies for a PTA bake sale. That sort of thing."

Amber nodded, watching the scenery pass by her window. The light snow she'd seen back in Bangor was heavier out here. It wasn't falling now, but the side of the road showed evidence of recent plowing.

"How much farther?" she asked. *Damn it*, she thought. *I wasn't going to ask that!*

"Not too much farther, really. We're making great time." He reached over and tapped a glove box in front of her. "Open that, will you?"

Curious, she pushed in the latch and pulled the compartment open. Inside sat a set of keys on a brass key ring with a small spaceship attached. Reaching inside, she grasped them and removed it before shutting the box again.

"Forgive the keyring," Larry laughed. "Amanda was a huge fan of scifi movies. I thought it best to keep them on that ring so I wouldn't lose them. You're welcome to change it out at any time."

She flipped through the ring. "What are they to?"

"Well, that's to your SUV. It's parked at the house." She must've looked shocked because he laughed at her. "You didn't think she didn't drive, did you? Amanda was old, yes. But she did things on her terms. In her way. If she could've, she would've driven herself to the funeral home after she died."

41

Chuckling, she replied, "I guess it just didn't occur to me that I'd end up with my own car from all of this. It's just…I don't know." She couldn't describe the feeling of freedom that encompassed her soul. She was going to live there for at least six months, yes. But she wasn't trapped.

"The others are to the front and back door, the carriage house, and the boat house. When you get to the house itself, you'll find more. She laid them out on a board, labeled most of them. Others, well, you'll have to find out what they go to."

"Carriage house? Boat house?"

"The house is old, historic. It dates back to the early 1800's. Instead of a garage, they had buildings where they could stable horses, keep a carriage or two. It was converted to a garage and storage decades ago. But the exterior remains the same." He paused, shifting in his seat. "The house is on the banks of the Allagash River. That's the main reason it's named The River House. There's a private dock and boat house. Amanda never kept a boat, said they were little more than a money pit. But it's there if you want to buy one at some point."

"What's the house like? I mean, is it big? Am I going to need to pay for repairs to it right away?"

"It's not small, no. Given the age, things do tend to go awry now and then. She's kept up on the painting and the roof. She had the interior completely renovated about fifteen years ago. Upgraded all the plumbing and electrical, but kept the small details that come with a house that's two centuries old. The detail in the woodwork, the built in cabinets, that sort of thing. Someone tried to talk her into removing the pocket doors but she wouldn't hear of it. Said it was part of the charm of the house. I think, all told, there's four bedrooms and three baths. Used to have more, but she said elbow room was important. Though she lived alone, so not sure who she thought needed the space."

He slowed down as a road appeared on the right, heading into a dense forested area. The small green sign read "Cavendish 25 miles." They were almost there.

"Larry, I'm anxious to see the house and all, but can we stop at a store first? I want to get settled and see everything before I make a big shopping trip, but I'd rather not live on take-out until then." She laughed.

He wagged a finger at her. "You're smart, young lady. I should've thought of that. No worries. We'll stop at the store, let you get what you need for a day or two. It's on the way anyhow."

Another few minutes and the houses began to appear. Some old, others looking fairly recently built. The speed limit dropped and Larry followed the road as it bent to the left. The vehicle crested a small hill, and she saw the town spread out in front of her. It wasn't big, no. But it was at least twice the size of Louden.

"Welcome home," Larry said.

Excitement seized her once again. She beamed at him and tightened her grip on the keys.

It didn't take long for them to pull into the parking lot of a grocery store. A few cars were scattered around the lot. Amber didn't expect it to be busy, not in early afternoon. And that was fine. The fewer people she met immediately, the better. She wanted to get settled in the house, find out some of the secrets Amanda had talked about, before she made friends.

The shopping went fairly quickly. She didn't want to get much, since she really had no idea what was there. Larry guided her, let her know the paper plates and plastic silverware weren't necessary. But microwave popcorn was just fine. In quick order, they were in line at the register.

"Hey, Larry! Glad to see you back in town!" the cashier called out as they approached. Darting out from behind her position, she gave him a quick hug. "Doug's been keeping your seat warm at the poker table."

Larry returned the embrace without embarrassment. "Great, Louise. May not make it tonight, though. We just got back into town and my wife'll kill me if I run off again that fast."

Amber quietly began to unload her purchases onto the conveyor belt.

"Oh, heavens! You must think I'm such a knucklehead. You must be Ms. Cross' heir!" Louise reached out a hand to Amber, expectation on her face.

Smiling briefly, she shook it. "Amber Cross," she said.

Louise moved back behind her register and began to ring up Amber's items. "Welcome, Amber! Do you mind if I call you Amber? If you do, just let me know. I'm great with names!" She chatted incessantly, fast enough that Amber didn't bother to try and reply. They hadn't had much to eat on the road, and it was starting to affect her. All Amber wanted to do was see her home, eat some food, and relax.

"Louise, it's a bit early to invite her to bingo night," Larry jumped in, startling Amber. She'd zoned out, completely unaware the woman had actually stopped talking.

"I'm sorry, Louise. It's been a long day," she muttered as she swiped her card. "It sounds great, and I'm sure I'll check it out sometime soon. Right now, though, I'd like to go home."

"Silly me," Louise answered. Was that pity that Amber saw on her face? She shrugged it off as the woman continued. "You must be exhausted with everything. You let me know if you need anything and I'll help you right away."

Larry began to scoop up the bags as Amber thanked her for her kindness. They silently loaded the groceries into the SUV. As soon as she was back in her seat, Amber let out a huge sigh.

"That was my fault," Larry said. "I should've checked to see if she was working when we first went in. Louise can be a bit much."

"It's okay," she let out another sigh. "I think all of *this*," she waved her hands around the car, "is finally getting to me. All I want to do right now is go home, eat, and take a nap."

Larry snapped his seat belt into place. "Well then, why don't we head out to The River House and let you do just that?" He turned the key in the ignition and pulled out of the parking lot.

She tried to get a feel for the layout of town. Shops, restaurants, and the like. After a few streets, though, she gave up. She'd figure out her way around eventually. After all, she had six months to do it. She shouldn't expect to learn where everything was as soon as she arrived.

"This is your street," Larry said as they made another left. "See that line of trees up ahead?" He pointed down the road. "That's the river."

Sitting up straight in her seat, Amber leaned forward. "Where's River House?" she asked.

He pointed to the large house at the end of the street. "Right there."

Her jaw dropped. Leaning forward, her hand touching the dashboard, she stared at the image coming ever closer.

The colonial was green with white trim. Shutters adorned all the windows. Two stately columns flanked the front door. Mentally, she started to count. "Two floors, or three?" she asked.

"Two, plus a full attic. There's also a finished basement that Amanda used for storage. I don't know what she did with the attic. She never showed me." Larry pulled the car into the driveway. Off to one side, a building stood. A covered walkway extended from it to the back of the house.

"Is that the carriage house?"

Larry put the car into park. "Yes. Your car's in there. The walkway was put in about the same time she remodeled the house. Said she got tired of having to shovel snow just to get her groceries inside."

Amber grabbed her keys, and her fingers fumbled with the seat belt in her haste. Larry was out and opening her door before she was unbuckled. "Welcome home, Ms. Cross," he said formally as he extended a hand to help her from the car.

She slid out of the car, staring at the house in awe. Four or more of her house in Texas could fit in that thing! And it was hers now.

"Go ahead and get inside, Amber. I'll get the luggage."

Grinning, she kept herself from running toward the door. It took her a few tries to find the right key. Sliding it into the lock, she turned it. The sound of the bolt moving aside thrilled her. She turned the knob and crossed the threshold.

Dark wood, polished and gleaming, ran underneath a floral rug. The pale yellow walls reflected the late afternoon sunlight. Sitting to one side, a bench rose from the floor. The sides of the bench rose, making a pair of small side tables while brass hooks lined either side of a polished mirror. The staircase dominated the hallway, curving upward. Two doors, one on each side of her, gave her even more choices. Which way to go and explore first? Not sure why, she caressed the banister. The wood felt warm, welcoming. A feeling of love, of acceptance, began to wash over her. Was the house alive and happy to see her?

"Kitchen's straight back and to the left if you want to get your food frozen again." Larry's voice broke the spell she was under.

"Oh, I, um. Sorry." She reached for some of the bags he was holding.

"It's fine. I'll go get the suitcases and all of that. If you don't mind, I'll just leave them here in the foyer. You've got the choice of bedrooms, after all." He disappeared back out the door.

Amber moved down the hallway, intent on getting the food put away before it went bad. The kitchen was designed well, with fairly new appliances. She dropped the bags on the island and began to unload them. Perishables went into the fridge and freezer, while the rest could stay on the counter. She wanted to make a good assessment of the supplies already in the house, but that wasn't going to happen today.

Her first impressions of the room, however, were favorable. It was clean, uncluttered. The microwave was built into a wall instead of taking up counter space. A knife block and coffee pot sat out. Above the island, a rack dropped down from the ceiling and held a variety of pots and pans. The afternoon light came streaming through a large window above the deep double sink. Hanging from the curtain rod was a strand of crystals that sent dozens of rainbows out across the room.

"Amber!" Larry called out. "That's the last of it. If you don't mind, I'm heading home. I'll call you in the morning to see how things are going."

"Thank you!" She called out in reply. She heard the heavy door shut as he left.

Leaning against the counter, she pulled a banana free from the bunch she'd bought. Peeling it, she smiled. It was her first meal in her new home. The exhaustion she'd felt earlier left, replaced by curiosity. It was time to find out just what the place was like.

Chapter Five

She wandered around the first floor, randomly touching pieces of furniture. It was tasteful, not overly ornate. A formal dining room, with a cabinet full of dishes and a long table. Big enough to have ten people around it for dinner. Sighing, she wondered if she'd ever even use the room. Maybe turn it into something a bit less formal. Amber really didn't see herself getting to know that many people well enough to host dinner. Besides, she had no clue how to even prepare such a meal.

A small bathroom hid underneath the staircase. Good. She wouldn't have to run upstairs all the time.

Half of the bottom of the house was taken over by the living area. The room itself was dominated by the huge fireplace. Given Larry's description of the snow up here being measured in feet, she realized she'd have to figure out how to use the thing. Wasn't she supposed to get the chimney swept or something, too? The last thing she wanted to happen to her new home was for it to go up in flames.

Wandering aimlessly back through the pocket doors near the front entry, she leaned against the framework. Her suitcases and shoeboxes, all neatly stacked and off to one side, reminded her she still had to unpack. Which meant choosing what room would be hers.

Scooping up a few of the boxes, she started up the staircase. A feeling of purpose swept over her. There would be plenty of time to explore the house properly. But she did need to take a bath or shower tonight. On the way up, she remembered how comfortable the bed on the plane had been. Surely, any mattresses here would be of the same quality. At least, she hoped so.

The staircase turned and she continued to climb. The wood floors remained silent beneath her feet. For a house as old as this one was, she'd expected at least a creaky step or two. The upstairs opened up as she climbed the last few steps. A hallway, doors on each side, and windows on each end, beckoned her. The late afternoon light filtered through a stained glass panel at the top of the west facing window, casting muted blues and greens on the dark wood floor. One side had four doors, the other two.

She blinked at the brightness and looked closer at the stained glass. Embedded in the panes was the same symbol in the necklace and wax seal. The image warmed her soul and she found herself smiling. Whatever it meant, it had to be good.

Turning her head, she looked at the window on the opposite end. The five pointed star and 'C' rested there as well.

The corner of one of the boxes bit into her arm, reminding her of her task. The door on the far end of the hall beckoned. "Trust my instincts," she whispered, and strode toward the door. This was her home now, and she had to stop being afraid of it.

Balancing the boxes in one arm, she turned the knob and opened the door. Her free hand felt along the wall, finding the light switch and flipping it up. Warm light bathed the room.

A large, four-poster canopy bed dominated the room. Fabric fell from the top, pulled aside and tied with cord on each post. A long dresser and mirror sat against one wall. A pair of nightstands sat on each side of the bed, each tucked neatly beneath a window. On the padded bench at the end of the bed sat a remote. Glancing around, she saw the large flat screen TV mounted on one wall. Two doors led from the room on the opposite one. She placed the boxes on the bench, near the remote, and went to check behind the doors.

One opened into a short corridor, with cabinets lining each side. Amber pulled open drawers and doors at random, finding a mix of bed linens, blankets, and towels. The arched opening at the other end put her into a large master bath. A massive claw-foot tub sat underneath the window. A small dressing table sat off to one side.

She retraced her steps slowly, intent on opening the other door. *Probably a closet*, she thought to herself. But she wanted to check. As she walked back into the bedroom, she saw the envelope sitting on the dresser. The same paper as had been used on the note she was given on the plane.

Curious, she picked it up and moved toward the bed. Turning it over, the wax seal was unbroken. She lowered herself onto the bed and broke the seal. Pulling the letter out, she read:

My dear one,

I've left you several notes around the house, like this one. You'll find them when they're ready to be found. Do not worry if you can't find them, or they seem to appear from nowhere. Sometimes, the only way to truly find that what we need the most is not to be looking for it.

This is now your home. Not mine. Do not, I beg you, hesitate to remove things that were mine that you no longer need. Like a closet full of clothes, or a dresser full of granny panties.

In the room across the hall from this one, you'll find some boxes and packing tape. Do not hesitate to pack up anything you don't like or won't use. This is, I repeat, your home now. It should reflect your tastes, not mine.

Up here is also the office, study, library, whatever your generation calls it these days. On the desk, you'll find a small notebook full of business cards. Call Emily with Secondhand Treasures. She's a wonderful woman. Let her know you have clothing to donate and she'll come pick it all up. It's a commission-based store, but she's just as likely to hand out whatever a family needs if they've experienced a disaster as to sell it. I never took cash. Told her to donate whatever was my cut to the local food bank. It's your choice if you want to do the same.

I think that's it for now. I'm sure you'll be busy for the next few days, getting settled into your home. But don't forget to get to the grocery store and stock up. Winter around here can happen suddenly.

With love,

Amanda

P. S. The cat's name is Minerva.

Amber blinked. *What cat?* she thought, mouthing the words. Not that she'd mind having one around. It was on the list of things she'd never had as a kid growing up.

The door opened a little more and a calico cat sauntered in. Green eyes considered Amber as the creature leaped onto the bench. She sniffed the boxes, rubbing one furry cheek against the edge before jumping on the bed near Amber.

"Are you Minerva?" Amber asked.

The cat sat down, her tail curling across her paws, and meowed.

Amber held out a hand, allowing the cat to sniff her. A loud purring began to rumble from Minerva's chest as she tilted her head.

Laughing, Amber gave the cat some quick scratches around her ears. "Well, Minerva. It looks like we're roomies. Shall we start to get the house in order?"

Blinking once, the cat lay down and went to sleep. Smiling, Amber rose from the bed and went in search of the boxes mentioned in the letter.

Chapter Six

*A*mber sighed, staring at the nearly empty fridge. "Well, Minerva, I don't think I can wait any longer. I've got to get us some food." She closed the door and looked down.

The cat meowed at her once. To Amber, it was almost an agreement.

Pulling open a drawer, she snatched up a pad of paper and pen. There was still some cat food on a shelf in the pantry, and she wanted to make sure she got the brand Minerva was used to.

She scanned the contents, making note of staples that were running low. Then added items she liked to eat and knew how to cook. Finally, she dug out a cookbook. She'd peeked inside already, and earmarked a few recipes that sounded good and wouldn't be hard for her to make. Adding the last few items to her list, she tore off the sheet and replaced the pad and pen in the drawer.

Folding up the list, she tucked it into the back pocket of her jeans as she strode toward the front of the house. Shoving her feet into the snow boots near the front door, she grabbed at her coat hanging from a hook. She paused to comb her hair with her fingers quickly. Shrugging the coat on, she picked up her purse and keys. "Back in a jiffy, Minerva. Be good while I'm gone!" she called out as she walked out the door.

Locking it behind her, she realized she'd gone out the front door instead of the back. It'd been snowing the last couple of days. The fresh, white powder stood between her and the carriage house. Glancing to her right as she broke a path, she sighed as the enclosed walkway came into view. At least she'd remember to go that way when she got home.

She found the key to the side door and walked into the garage. It'd been a busy few days. Organizing things to go to the consignment shop, unpacking her own items, getting into some sort of routine to it all. Amanda had left a list of passwords for the computer and laptop, so she'd been able to order some things online. Finding the music system was great. Just a few pushes of a button and she had music all over the house while she moved around. It was a good thing she liked retro or classic rock, as the CD collection was full of some of the best albums ever. Some things came on that she'd never heard before, but rarely did she find something she'd remove and put aside to donate.

Moving around to the driver's side of the SUV, Amber unlocked the car and got inside. Taking a few moments, she familiarized herself with the controls. On the visor above her was a remote. Clicking the button, she heard the mechanism for the garage door begin to move. She started the car and put it into reverse, backing out slowly.

The snow wasn't deep. Not yet, anyway. She'd gotten in the habit of watching the newscast in the evening, paying close attention to the weather forecast. A storm was coming later in the week. She considered buying extra food than what was on her list just in case.

Once she was clear of the garage, she pushed the remote again to close the door and put the car into drive.

That was something else she'd been doing. Learning the layout of Cavendish from the internet. The last thing she needed was to get lost the minute she left her front door. It was only three wrong turns before she pulled into the parking lot of the grocery store.

It was busier than normal, with lots of residents trying to stock up before the storm. Parking her car, she slung her purse across her body and headed into the store.

Shopping was going fine, until she encountered one ingredient on her list. It was for a stew she wanted to try.

Something she could put together and let simmer all day, plus give her lots of leftovers for the freezer. Staring at the endless racks of spices, she bit her lip in frustration. Why couldn't she find the right type of pepper?

"Need some help?" a male voice asked.

Jumping, Amber spun. For just a moment, she feared it was Bruce. But the face smiling at her wasn't him. This man was friendly, with dark hair and green eyes. And handsome enough to make her heart skip a beat.

"I, um, yeah," she laughed. "I can't seem to find the right type of pepper for this stew I wanted to try." She pointed to the list in her hand. "Either I'm blind, or there's no such thing as wt pepper."

Leaning in, he read over her shoulder. "I think it's white pepper you're looking for," he said. She glanced down at her list, feeling dumb. "Here it is," he pulled a small tin off the shelf and handed it to her.

"Thanks," she blushed. "I was in a rush when I made my list. Can't even decipher my own handwriting." She laughed a little.

"It's fine, really. I learned how to cook from my grandma. And her handwriting was atrocious." He smiled again and held out his hand. "I'm Heath. Heath Morrisy."

"Amber Cross," she replied, shaking it.

Heath started, "Cross? Are you related to Amanda?"

She nodded. "Yes. She was my great-aunt."

"You're the new resident of The River House, then? I'd heard someone new had taken over the place." He pulled out his wallet and removed a business card. "Not sure if she kept this, but here's my card." He handed it to her.

Glancing at the card, she read, "Morrisy Handyman Services." She remembered seeing a card similar in design in Amanda's book.

"I used to help her out with the house a lot. Make sure the furnace kept heating the place, yard work, that sort of thing. I've been meaning to come by but haven't had time. Amanda had me doing the Halloween decorating outside of the house the last few years. I didn't know if you'd like the same sort of help."

Amber's eyes flew open wide, "Oh, no! Halloween! I completely forgot and Larry…sorry, Mr. Dixon…told me it was always such a big deal for her. That the kids here in town totally got a kick out of everything she did." She looked at her cart. "At least I can get some candy while I'm here."

"Would you like me to come by this weekend? Help you decorate? I mean, I understand if you don't, but I know where she kept everything and all that."

She sighed, "Actually, I'd love that. I've been so busy trying to get unpacked and learn where things are in the house, I haven't got a clue where the decorations would be stored." She laughed again. "I don't even know if there's a snowblower in the garage or if I'll have to shovel by hand."

Heath laughed. "No worries. The decorations were made to withstand a white Halloween. I'll be there on Saturday. Ten a.m. work for you?"

She nodded. "That works fine. Minerva tends to wake me up by seven to feed her."

His face lit up. "Minerva's back? I heard Isabel Andrews talking about feeding her." She must've looked puzzled at his statement. Laughing, he went on, "Isabel and her family live on the same street you do. Just a few houses down. She's a big cat person, so it doesn't surprise me that Minerva went there when Amanda died. It's good to know she went home, though."

Amber caught a glance out the front windows of the store. The day was fading fast, and she wanted to get back home before dark if she could. "I've got to finish shopping and get home," she held up his card. "Thanks for this, and the help on Saturday. Oh, and with the pepper!" She waved at him as she pushed her cart around the corner.

She finished her shopping and headed to the register. The cashier who had been so friendly when she arrived was working. Something told her not to go through her line, though. Louise seemed almost too friendly, too eager to get to know her. And she wasn't past looking over her shoulder yet.

The plane she'd been on had been on the news. Well, the wreckage was. Her parents and Bruce, posing as the grieving fiancée, gave out a few interviews. Her gut told her he wasn't buying it, though. Until he had her body in a coffin, he'd never believe she was dead.

She made small talk with her cashier, mainly about the approaching storm. It wasn't long before she had everything loaded in the SUV and she was heading back home.

Driving down the main street, a store sign caught her eye. Promising herself she would only peek, she found a parking spot and went inside.

A musky aroma filled the small shop. An odd assortment of crystals, books, and herbs intermixed with fantasy art and racks with handmade clothing in natural fibers filled the place.

"You're her great-niece, aren't you?"

Amber turned toward the sound of the voice. A woman, not much older than herself, stood behind a counter. Her smile reached her blue eyes. "I didn't mean to startle you. I don't think anyone's mentioned how much like Amanda you truly look." She walked around the corner, holding out her hand in greeting. "I'm Kate. Amanda used to come in here often."

Shaking the woman's hand, Amber smiled back. A small pentacle, with a crescent moon woven between the lines of the star, decorated her neck. "You're Wiccan, then?"

"Yes, I am. No coven, though. Amanda and I had that in common. Neither of us felt a need to have others around us when we talked with our Goddesses. Some do, but not us." Kate looked Amber up and down, the gaze making her feel like this woman was seeing something she didn't.

"You're still afraid. Good. He's not done hunting you yet. The time will come. Sooner than you may want. But you will defeat him. You're not alone."

Blinking, Amber whispered, "How do you know about Bruce?"

Kate shrugged, the dark curls bobbing on her shoulders. "People leave a mark on us. If we're lucky, it's good. They're willing to accept us for who we are, even if that means we're not part of their life. Others, well, let's just say they don't play nice with others." She smiled, the mood in the room shifting. "So, Amanda told me you were going to choose a new name. May I ask what it is?"

"Amber. Amber Cross." She smiled in return.

"Welcome to Cavendish, Amber. And to my humble shop. The Cauldron is open to all, regardless of faith. If you're to follow a Path, you will find it on your own. All I can provide you is friendship and a sounding board." She glanced outside. "The storm's approaching. I need to head home, as do you. I know Amanda had my card in her book. If you can, let me know you got home safe. I would not want any harm to come to you, my friend."

"Are we friends?" Amber's voice was quiet. She felt a desperate need for a friend in her new home.

"If you wish, yes. But get going. Minerva's going to be worried about you." Kate began to lead Amber toward the door.

"You know about the cat? How?"

"I visited Amanda often, and had a good relationship with Minerva. Besides, every witch needs a cat." She opened the door to the shop.

The cold wind hit Amber with a force. Kate was right. The storm wasn't far off. "I'm not a witch. Am I?"

"That's up to you to discover, Amber. Wiccans do not recruit like other faiths. It is up to you to decide which Path is right for you, not me."

Amber nodded and darted out of the shop. The wind picked up, the gust threatening to pull the knit hat off her head. The snow began to fall, heavy and fast. With one hand on her head, the keys in the other, she dashed for her car.

She pulled into the carriage house, waiting to make sure the door lowered behind her before she turned off the car. Kate's warning about Bruce had her on edge. She let out a deep breath and got out.

Her arms loaded with bags, she managed to get the tailgate closed. The beep of the lock response echoed slightly in the room. Her feet started toward one door, then she stopped. Remembering the enclosed walkway, she headed toward another one.

The short walk was dark, but she was grateful for the cover with every step. The wind rattled the panes of plexiglas. Snow was already starting to pile up on the river side. She walked quickly to the back door, the key in one hand.

Unlocking the door, she darted inside and past the mudroom into the kitchen. Easing the bags onto the center island, she retraced her steps. She shut the back door, locking both the normal lock and the deadbolt, then headed to the front entry to get rid of her boots and the rest of her outer wear.

The street lights illuminated the thick blanket of white. The fresh powder sparkled in a magical way. Amber smiled. She'd never seen snow growing up, let alone this much. While she was fairly certain she'd be sick of it by the time the six months were up, it mesmerized her now.

Minerva watched her, the furry tail swishing back and forth slowly across the floor, as she put the groceries away. "Just a few more minutes," Amber told the cat. As soon as the perishables were put away, she fed her. Once the cupboards were restocked and the bags stored, she opened the can of soup she'd left on the counter for her own dinner. Dumping the contents into another container, she put it in the microwave. While it warmed up, she remembered that Kate wanted to know she arrived home safely.

She finished her dinner prep, poured the steaming hot soup into a bowl, and added a spoon. Making sure her cell was still tucked into her back pocket, she made her way upstairs.

The book of cards sat on the desk up in the office, on the same side of the house as her bedroom. Balancing the bowl in one hand, she twisted the handle with the other one. Opening the door, she flipped the light switch.

She hadn't changed much in this room, and didn't plan to. The desk sat in the perfect place, underneath the corner windows. Floor to ceiling bookcases lined almost the entirety of the room. One shelf could move, leading to a passage that led directly to the walk-in closet in the bedroom. A rolling ladder system made it easy to reach the books on the top shelves.

The shelves themselves weren't overstocked. Eclectic bookends decorated open spaces, keeping the books from falling over. History seemed to be a favorite subject of Amanda's, along with fantasy novels. About half of the collection, however, were occult or Wiccan in theme. Mythology, ritual casting, spell books, and herbalism intermixed with the rest.

Careful not to spill the contents, she placed the bowl on the desk. Amber sank into the leather office chair and watched as Minerva climbed on the top of the cat tree nestled in a corner. She pulled her phone out of her pocket while reaching for the small leather book of cards. Thumbing through it, she located the one for The Cauldron and dialed the number.

It went to her voicemail, so Amber left a brief message and hung up. The snow continued to fall outside. Picking up her bowl, her eyes scanned the shelves as she ate.

One book looked out of place. While there was a mix of subjects, they tended to be grouped together. The fiction, for example, wasn't on the same shelf as the religious books.

There was no writing on the leather binding. From where she sat, it had no fraying on the ends. The surrounding books were all historical, and had a title on the spine. Curious, she put down the almost empty bowl and crossed the room.

Pulling it off the shelf, she could tell it was old. Books simply weren't created like this anymore. Leather, hardcover, with pages that weren't cleanly cut. In fading gold letters, a title stood out on the front cover.

"'The Guardians of Charon and the River Styx.'"

No author was listed. She opened the book. There was no publisher, author, or copyright date listed. The opening sentences made a chill run down her spine.

The River Styx has many waystations. Each one must be manned by a Guardian. These people serve as both guides to the souls who must ride the ferry, and guard Charon from those who would destroy his world.

The phone rang, startling her. Putting the book down, she grabbed at the phone. Larry's name and number flashed at her. "Hey, Larry," she said as she answered the phone.

"Hi, Amber! Just wanted to make sure you were okay. This storm's going to last for a while. We've had the power flicker some, too." His concerned voice made her smile.

"Be sure to tell her we'll come get her if she's scared!" Amber heard a female voice in the background.

Larry laughed, "My wife wants to make sure you know we can come rescue you if you need us to."

"I'm fine so far. I went to the store earlier today and stocked up. Minerva's not even concerned. She's napping."

"Good. If you do lose power, give me a call. I can set up the generator if you need me to."

"There's a generator?"

"Yes. Amanda bought one several years ago, right before a really bad storm. It's stored in a locked box just out from the back door. Should be plenty of gas in it, and there's probably a few more full cans out in the carriage house if you run out."

Amber remembered one really bad winter back in Louden. Her house was without power for several days. Her mom was so upset about having to live in "primitive conditions like some trash family" that her father bought the first generator they could find. Which instantly became her responsibility to make sure it would work properly at a moment's notice. "I've dealt with generators before, Larry. Good to know there's one outside. I may have to shovel snow to reach it, but I won't go cold."

As if on cue, the lights flickered. "And I might need it before I know it," she laughed. "Tell your wife thank you for her concern, but I'll be fine. I'll call you tomorrow if you want me to. Oh, before I forget!" She fished the handyman's card out of her other pocket. "Do you know a Heath Morrisy?"

"Yes, decent guy. Used to help Amanda around the house. Why?"

"I met him at the grocery store tonight. He offered to come over and help me set up the Halloween display on

Saturday morning. Just wanted to see what you thought of him."

"He's someone Amanda trusted, if that helps. Have you met anyone else in town yet?"

"Kate, from The Cauldron. Don't even know why I went into the shop today. She said she and Amanda were good friends."

"I know she's Wiccan, like Amanda was. If you're interested in the faith, I'm sure she'll put you on the right Path. Amanda always spoke highly of her. She was a frequent guest in The River House." He paused, "In fact, she had Kate summoned to do a Sending when she was near death. Amanda wouldn't allow just anyone to do that."

There was that word again. Path. Quickly, she said goodnight to Larry and hung up her phone. Was this where she was supposed to be? Was she finally traveling down the road she was always meant to?

A small voice inside her head told her yes. Everything she'd gone through since she'd left her parent's house felt more right than anything else in her life up to that point.

The lights flickered again. Remembering the flashlight sitting on one of the bookshelves, she grabbed it. Picking up the soup bowl, she headed back downstairs.

The book lay on the desk, forgotten.

Chapter Seven

"Meow."

Amber groaned, one arm coming out from under the heavy quilts.

"Meow."

Minerva's furry face rubbed against hers, her whiskers tickling her nose. Opening her eyes, the cat regarded her with an even stare.

"Meow."

Giving up, Amber reached up and scratched the cat between her ears. "Fine. I'll feed you." Pushing aside the covers, she slid her feet into a pair of fluffy slippers. She grabbed at the thick robe she'd left draped across the bench and followed the cat downstairs.

She'd managed to keep the power throughout the storm and the ice that followed for the next two days. The drifts of snow against the back side of the house were almost up to the window sills. And they were now covered with an icy sheen.

After she fed Minerva, she started to get some coffee brewing. The clock on the microwave told her it was almost 8:30 a.m. She had to hurry if she was going to try and get the walkway cleared before Heath showed up.

While the coffee pot did its job, she darted upstairs and got dressed. She ran a brush through her hair. It was growing out already. When the roads were cleared, she'd have to find a local salon.

Once she was dressed, she went back downstairs. She figured she had time for at least one cup of coffee before getting to work. Pouring a steaming mug, she added sugar and cream before heading to the living room.

Settling in on the couch, she picked up the remote and found the morning news. At least the weather forecast was favorable. Cold, yes, but no new storms coming for a few days. She'd have time to dig out the generator box.

Finishing her coffee, she turned the television back off. Minerva sat on a cat tree, cleaning her paws. Amber went back into the kitchen and put her mug in the sink, then headed toward the front door.

She pushed her feet into the snow boots while sliding her arms through the thick, puffy coat.

She shoved her keys in her coat pocket, pulled her hat on her head, and slid on her gloves. Absently, she thought she really needed to move this process to the mud room off the kitchen. Or get a second set of everything to make things faster.

Pausing as she went past the kitchen, she had a thought. It made little sense for the house keys to be the same everywhere. There was a board, just on the inside of the pantry. It had even more keys, all with labels. Opening the door, she scanned the small white disks attached to each one. "Aha!" she proclaimed as she spied one marked "Carriage House storage." She removed it from the hook and slid it in the opposite pocket so she didn't drop it when she pulled out her house keys.

Heading out to the carriage house, she watched the river for a moment. Small chunks of ice bobbed on the surface, the current moving them at a steady pace. Maybe in the spring, she'd go check out the boathouse.

Amber unlocked the door. Swinging it open, she flipped on the light switch. While there was room for her car and another, both sides had enclosed storage areas. There was also a ladder leading up to a loft storage area. *One day*, she promised herself. Much like the boat house, exploring would wait for warmer weather.

"Okay," she said aloud, her breath coming out in steamy clouds. "If I was a shovel or snow blower, where would I be kept?" The area for the cars was tidy. No empty hooks, gas cans, or yard care items. If there was a shovel or such, it had to be in one of the locked areas.

Shrugging, Amber moved to the door closest to her. Pulling out the spare key, she slid it into the deadbolt and turned the lock. The lock popped open. Moving aside the hasp, she opened the door.

A variety of yard tools, all neatly lined on walls and shelves, rested inside. Rakes, shovels, pruning shears along with other items. A snow shovel was near the door. Just below it sat a gas-powered snow blower. She tilted the device and backed it out of the shed.

Clicking on the switch near the door, she waited for the garage door to open. It didn't take long for her to figure out how to work the machine. It came to life with a roar and she began to clear a path from the building to the street.

An hour later, most of the work was done. She'd be able to get out if she wanted to drive somewhere. The front walkway and sidewalk were clear, as well. Remembering bags of salt were in the shed, she moved the blower back to its resting spot and grabbed the handles of a wheelbarrow. Flinging the de-icer into it, she scooped up a large spreader off a shelf. Methodically, she began to spread the mixture on the freshly cleared ground. The last thing she needed was to have a child slip and fall on Halloween.

"Great idea!" a voice called out.

Startled, Amber raised her head. Heath walked up the driveway. "I was going to recommend doing that, but it looks like you beat me to it."

She paused, smiling at him. "Well, the last thing I need right now is a trick-or-treater taking a fall because of ice."

He nodded, "Smart. Not everyone in town thinks of it. Usually hear about some kid who ended up with a broken arm or bruised ego from taking a slide in costume." He glanced to the open carriage house. "Amanda kept all of the decorations in there." He pointed a heavily gloved finger towards the building. "If you're ready, I'll get started."

She shrugged. "Works for me. Do you need me to unlock one of the storage areas?"

"No, she had it all up in the loft. Shouldn't take long." He waved at her and walked away.

Amber went back to spreading the salt, taking her time.

The morning went fast. She kept focused on making things safe, while Heath set up the various decorations. Some of them were comical, others bordered on props from a zombie movie. "Glad I'm seeing them in the daylight for the first time," she said.

Heath leaned on one particularly gruesome figure. "Eh, this here is Fred. He's a favorite among the kids. He looks scary, but tends to have a high pitched laugh that gives them fits." He glanced around the yard. "I think I got it all. Only thing left is Matilda. Amanda always had me plant her in someplace new each year. We've got families who bring their kids that remember that particular witch from their own childhood. Finding her spot for the year has been a decades long game of hide and seek."

"Really? Well, that's a tradition I don't dare tamper with. What does she look like?"

Heath removed the lid of a plastic storage bin and pulled out a shoebox. Lifting the lid, he said, "This is Matilda."

Inside rested a small doll. Spiky red hair jutted out from underneath a conical black hat. The painted porcelain face was at peace, eyes closed. She grasped a broom in her hands. Flowing robes of black and white finished the outfit. There was a subtle print on the fabric. Pulling the doll closer, she saw the outline of a pentacle interlaced with a 'C'. The familiar symbol made her smile. Amber looked up at Heath. "Surely she shouldn't be out in the weather.

Somewhere inside, I think." She looked up, her soul searching along with her eyes. A window upstairs, directly above the front porch. She knew it was one of the guest rooms. Someplace she hadn't explored much. But it was also the doll's home. "Up there, center window."

"Morning, miss. Morning, Heath." A male voice called out.

Turning, she saw the mailman walking up to the two of them. "Hello," she said.

"Getting all decorated? Hannah'll be so excited." The man smiled as he rifled through a pile of mail.

"Hannah?" Amber asked.

He looked up. "Sorry, that's my daughter. She's eight going on twenty-three. Was sad when she learned Ms. Cross passed away." He handed her a small pile, "Oh, let me find a pen. One needs to be signed for."

Amber flipped through the envelopes and found it. The return address was Louden. And it was addressed to Grace Adams.

Her stomach plummeted. "I'm sorry," she stammered. "This one doesn't belong to me." She held the envelope back out to the mailman. "My name's not Grace Adams. It's Amber...Amber Cross."

The man shrugged and took the envelope from her. "Okay, sorry about that. I'll make sure it gets sent back as refused."

"Here, let me do the honors." Heath stepped forward. He took the pen from the mailman and scribbled on the envelope, making sure Amber saw what he wrote.

"Return to sender. No such person at this address."

The postman took the letter, nodded once to them as he slipped it back into his bag, and walked off.

"Heath, I really appreciate your help this morning. But I, ah, I've got to make a phone call." She knew she was shaking. Larry needed to know about the letter, and fast.

"That's fine. I'll put everything away out here, lock up the carriage house for you." He leaned down and put the lid back on the storage bin.

"Thank you." She started to turn toward the house, then looked back at him. "What do I owe you?"

He lifted the bin in both hands. "Nothing. You did the hard work before I even got here. Maybe a cup of coffee when you're done taking care of things?"

She smiled. "I'd like that. Can I call you later then, get it set up?"

His grin got even bigger. "It's a date. Whenever you're ready."

She waved at him and went into the house.

As soon as she shut the door behind her, she collapsed. Sliding down the door, she tried to control her breathing. Had Bruce found her? Was it her parents? Her mind blindly went back over the news reports she'd seen after Ms. Cole ditched the plane. What could've gone wrong?

Frantically, she pulled off her gloves and threw them aside. Digging her cell out, she found Larry's number and dialed it.

"Hello?"

"Larry, it's Amber. Something's wrong. He found me." Tears crept into her voice.

"What? How?" he asked, concern in his voice.

"The mailman just came by. Had a registered letter from Louden. It was addressed to Grace Adams." Minerva came up and nestled into Amber's lap. Absently, she began to stroke the cat's fur. The cat responded with a calming purr.

"Did you take it?" his voice was insistent.

Shaking her head, she replied, "No. Heath was here, helping with the decorating. He put something about no one by that name at this address on the envelope. The mailman left with it."

Larry muttered something under his breath. "Okay, where are you now?"

"In the house. Minerva has me pinned." She sniffled.

"Okay. You met Kate, right?"

"Yes. I liked her."

"Good. I thought you might. Give her a call, see if she can come be with you for a bit. You can trust her, Amber. She'll get you calmed down. I'm going to try and track down the letter, make a few calls. I'll come see you when I have any information."

She sniffed again, the worst of the panic subsiding. "What if it's Bruce? What if the plane crash didn't convince him?"

"Trust me, Amber. Even if it is him, you have more friends here than you know. He will not drag you down with him." Larry's calm assurance felt good to hear. "Now, hang up and call Kate. Make some tea or coffee. Give Minerva some catnip. She really likes that stuff."

Laughing, Amber hung up the phone. She looked down at the cat in her lap. "You like catnip, huh? I do remember seeing a jar of the stuff in the pantry."

Minerva placed one paw on her cheek, as if to tell Amber things were going to be fine. With a flick of her bushy tail, she jumped off of Amber's lap and sauntered down the hall. Meowing for Amber to follow the whole way.

Chapter Eight

Charon comes, to ferry the souls
Take your seat, he knows where to go
The Ferryman knows the sum of your life
Take this coin, pay him when you arrive

The words leaped from the page, burning into Amber's very soul. She didn't know why, but they were important. She'd picked up the book she left on the desk after the last trick-or-treater was gone.

Her phone rang, making her jump. Grabbing at the screen, she saw Kate's number pop up. "How many did you get?" Amber asked as she answered the phone.

Kate laughed on the other end. "I lost count! I gave out tons of candy at the store, and even more when I got home. I know I had some repeat customers, though. How about you? How was your first Halloween in Cavendish?"

"I liked it! I was really surprised at how many parents were trying to find the doll. The kids were all so cute, too. Heath did a great job with the outdoor display. It really kept them on edge, wondering what they'd encounter next."

"Glad to hear it. I'm going to let you go. It's late, and I've got to be up early and in the shop tomorrow. Samhain's a few days away yet, but there's orders to fill and get shipped if they're going to arrive in time."

"Do you need a hand? I'm not doing anything tomorrow. It'd be fun to come in and help out." Amber said.

Kate hesitated. "Sure, if you're up to it. Tonight's a full moon, though. You may be up later than you expect. The light shines pretty bright. It may keep you up."

"I'll be fine," Amber replied. "About to head to bed anyway. See you in the morning!" She pressed the button to disconnect the call.

She put the book back on the desk and rose, moving toward the window. Scratching at Minerva's ears, she looked out. Kate was right. The moonlight on the snow was a brilliant white. A ribbon of inky blackness winding through the landscape, the river ran dark. There was no way you wouldn't know something was there, even without lights.

She went through the moving bookcase, taking the shortcut to the closet. Quickly, she changed into some flannel pajamas and fuzzy slippers. "I'm going to make sure it's all locked up downstairs again," she called out to Minerva as she moved back through the office.

As she got to the last few steps, she saw the bowl of candy sitting on the small table near the front door. She checked the locks, then grabbed the bowl. Heading to the back of the house, she double-checked the other entry. She walked into the kitchen, ready to stash the left over candy in the freezer.

"Hello," a woman's voice called out.

Amber dropped the bowl. The plastic rang hollowly as it hit the wood floor and candy scattered. She pulled a knife out of the block on the counter as she turned around.

An older woman sat on a stool at the island. She looked a lot like Amber, but something wasn't right.

She could see the entrance to the butler's pantry through the woman.

"Who? What?" she stammered.

The apparition smiled. "I'm sorry if I startled you, my dear. It's never easy to be introduced to a spirit for the first time. Necessary, yes. But not easy." The woman glanced around the kitchen. "I like some of the changes you've made. It's your house now, not mine. It should reflect that."

"You're Amanda?" Amber whispered.

She sighed. "I was. Now, who knows? I know more of who you are, what your Path should be, than my own."

Amber leaned against the counter, still clutching the knife. "Tell me. I only know this house, the inheritance, came at the precise time I needed to escape. If there's a reason for me to be here, I want to know what it is."

"I suppose I owe you that much. Why don't you put down the knife and get some coffee? The blade won't hurt me, and I won't hurt you. And coffee will make things easier to understand."

Amber looked at the knife in her hand. She'd grabbed it on instinct, but it was painfully obvious that it wouldn't do a thing to Amanda. She slid it back into the block. "Okay, that's reasonable. But you need to start talking while I brew."

"What name did you take? I doubt you kept the insipid one your parents foisted on you."

She drew a breath and slowly let it out, trying to calm down. She was having a conversation with a ghost! "Amber. I went with Amber Cross. Larry said you had no direct descendants and was the last with the surname, so it seemed appropriate." She opened the cupboard and pulled out a mug. "You were a witch, though. And now you're a ghost. Why didn't you know that already?"

"Wiccan, dear, not a witch precisely. And being Wiccan or a ghost doesn't mean we can read minds or eavesdrop on people." Her tone shifted, almost scolding Amber. "Thank you for the name, Amber. It means a great deal to know I'm not the last Cross after all."

"You're stalling. You said you knew who I was, what my Path would be." She finished getting the machine set up and turned back to Amanda, her arms crossed.

"This house has been inhabited for centuries. Sometimes by a man, other times a woman. Families have been raised here. And, despite anything shown to the world beyond this threshold, at least one occupant has always been Wiccan. The same applies to you. You may not know it yet, may not be ready to dedicate yourself to a particular Goddess, but you've started walking the Path already. If you hadn't, you wouldn't help Kate tomorrow in her shop."

"I thought you didn't eavesdrop?"

"Touché, Amber." She smiled. "I don't. I was on the way upstairs to greet you and heard you on the phone with Kate. I was hoping to see Minerva one more time. She was a good companion for me. I miss her greatly." A sadness clouded her face for a moment. "When I heard you hang up, I thought you might be changing. I knew that wouldn't be a good first introduction, so I came back down here. And waited."

The espresso machine hissed as the last drops of coffee made it through the brewer and into the cup. Amber turned, removed the cup, and turned off the machine. Moving toward the fridge for the milk she said, "Keep going."

"The reason there's always been a Wiccan in the house is that there's more to this place than most know. Indeed, only the Guardians know all of it. If you were to marry, have children, they would never learn the secret. Unless one was to succeed you at your post."

"Wait…Guardians? What were you guarding?"

Amanda rose. "Come. It's almost time and you will not believe me until you see it yourself." She moved toward the back door.

Amber put the cup down on the counter, curious. She turned the corner and stared out the huge windows that dominated the outer wall of the mud room.

The backyard shifted, the snow disappearing. The river moved closer. Black sand glistened in the moonlight, broken only by a small wooden dock. The river, shrouded in mist, lapped at the banks.

"Charon comes, to ferry the souls," Amber whispered.

"Exactly, my dear. You are here to be his Guardian, give instruction to those souls who need to be ferried to the underworld."

Amber turned to the ghost next to her, "Tonight, that's you." Her voice was hushed.

Nodding, her great aunt replied. "Yes. I've known Charon for decades. Do not lie to him, for he will know it before the words leave your mouth. He will keep every secret you tell him. He will protect you, as well."

Amber blinked, shaking her head. *This has to be a dream*, she thought. Looking back out the windows, she saw the prow of a small boat emerge from the mist. It slid up to the end of the dock. A hooded figure stood at the back, his hands grasping a rudder.

This wasn't a dream. It was real.

"I don't have any coin to give you," she whispered.

"Never fear. I wouldn't leave the next Guardian unprepared. Go to the fireplace. Find the brick with a pentacle etched into it. You will be able to move it aside and find a hidden niche. Inside is a bag. Bring that to me," Amanda instructed.

Amber darted to the living room and flipped on the light closest to the fireplace. It took her a moment or two to find the right brick. She pushed on it several times before she found the right spot. With a soft grinding sound, the brick moved aside. Reaching into the hole, her fingers grasped a leather object. She pulled it out. The pouch was tied shut and heavy. Turning it over, she heard the musical jingle of coins hitting against each other. She pushed the brick back into place and headed back to Amanda.

"Found it," she said, holding the pouch aloft.

"Good. When we get to the edge of the dock, say the words and give me two coins. No more, no less. I'm his only passenger this time."

"There will be more?"

The ghost moved through the back door. Amber moved quickly to unlock it and follow.

The warmth struck her first. Not overly warm, but certainly not the cold the recent storms had brought with them. "Each full moon, the waystation appears. Some months, you won't have any souls. Others will see many. Only those who follow this Path will find their way to Charon's ferry. And he makes many stops each time. The soul goes to the location it chooses."

Amber jogged to stay up with Amanda as she crossed the dark sand to the short dock, and the boat gently bobbing at the end of it. A look of immense peace settled over her face, one that was becoming more real the closer she got to the pier. When she put her bare foot on the wood, she lost the last of the ghostly visage.

"Are you real now?" Amber asked.

Amanda turned to her and smiled. "I've always been real, child. Even if my body wasn't, my soul was. That's what sets you apart from those in your past. They are concerned with superficial things. Money, power, connections, appearances. As long as you're true to yourself, the rest is inconsequential. Be real, Amber. Not fake."

"Listen well to her, Guardian," a deep male voice called out.

Amber looked up and saw the man in the boat staring at her. Black hair, pulled back with a silver band at the nape of his neck. Deep blue eyes stared back at her. Those eyes looked into her very soul.

"Hello, my friend. I think you finally get to take me for that ride." Amanda called out across the seven feet of wood that lay between her and the Ferryman.

Charon looked at Amber again, nodding once. "You're leaving me now, aren't you?" Tears spilled from her eyes. "I never said thank you for all of this."

"My dear Amber, no thanks are needed. It was my time to move on. And yours to move forward. I've left you notes. You've found one or two already. I may not be here physically." Amanda squeezed Amber's hands, But I will never leave you here"—she touched her chest— "or here." She moved her finger to her forehead. "Death is but a part of the journey, the same as life. You will learn this as a Guardian."

Amber knew it was time. Ignoring the tears, she pulled open the pouch and removed out two coins. "Charon comes, to ferry your soul," She began to recite the words that she didn't realize she'd memorized.

When she was done, she placed the coins into Amanda's hand. She felt a final tear trickle down her face as she said goodbye to the woman who had saved her life.

The older woman gently wiped it away with a single finger. "All will be well, my dear. My turn on the Wheel is done for now, but your life is just beginning. Live it. Neither in fear nor in anger. Love those who you can, forgive those who cannot accept you for who you are, and dance every chance you get." Amanda turned and walked toward Charon's boat. Settling onto a seat, she blew a kiss to Amber.

Amber returned the gesture and stayed on the dock until the mist reclaimed the craft and its' occupants.

Returning to the house, she locked the door behind her again. She stood in the mud room, watching as the River Styx disappeared and the snow came back.

"Meow," Minerva called out as she rubbed against Amber's legs.

Looking down, she smiled. "Yes, Minerva. She's gone now." She bent down and picked up the cat. "Let's get the coins put back away and head to bed." Turning, she saw the bowl and candy sitting on the floor of the kitchen. Minerva purred in her arms. The candy could wait for tomorrow.

Chapter Nine
November

"Kate, the printer ran out of ink," Amber called out from the back room of the shop. "I'm on the last shipping label, too." She laughed.

Her friend came through the beaded curtain separating the stock room from the front of the store. "Here, I'll show you where I keep the spare cartridges." She pulled out a clear plastic bin from a shelf and placed it on a small counter near the printer. Opening the lid, she looked at Amber. "Black or color?" she asked.

Amber glanced at the icon displaying the printer status on the desktop screen. "It's asking for black, but color's getting low as well."

Kate pulled out a cartridge and set it on top of the desk. "I'll wait. I rarely use the color, so I wait until the last possible minute to change it. Those get pricey fast." She put the lid back on the container. "Can you change it out or do you need me to show you how?" she asked as she slid the bin back into the right shelf.

"I've got it. This model's close to one I've used before." Amber rose from the computer chair and started to open the printer. "When does the shipping company show up?"

"Usually not before three." The bell over the front door chimed out. "If that's him, I'll stall him while you get the last order packed up." Kate left the back room.

Moving quickly, Amber changed out the ink cartridge and started to print the last label. As soon as it came out, she pulled the paper from the tray and put it on the final package. Kate had warned her that there were lots of orders to fill. She'd been in the back room packing boxes and printing shipping labels almost nonstop since ten that morning.

She put the last box on top of the others and slid the flat part of the hand cart underneath the stack. Pulling back on the handle, she tilted the load and began to back out of the stock room, intent on placing the outgoing shipments near the register to make pick up easier.

"That's great, Amber. Right there is perfect," Kate called out.

"Do I get to steal her for some coffee now?" Heath's voice startled her.

Amber glanced over her shoulder as she finished positioning the stack of boxes. "Hey, Heath! I'd love some coffee, if Kate can spare me."

"Go," she laughed. "You've been going nonstop since you got here! I love the help—the customers will get their orders in time. Now, get out of the shop and have some fun!" She all but shoved Amber to the door.

Grinning, she said, "Okay, fine. Let me grab my coat and purse." Diving once more into the back room, she lifted the coat off the peg and snagged her purse. "Is there a coffee shop close by," she asked as she came out to the main shop, "or are we driving?"

Heath nodded, "Nothing's that far away in Cavendish, really. At least, not in the summer months. Wait until then. Unless you're doing a big shopping trip, you won't drive for a week or more." He smiled, "To answer your question, though, there's a great spot just across the street. Great coffee, and even better food if you're hungry."

Amber's stomach growled loudly at the mention of food. "I've been betrayed!" she said in mock horror. Waving goodbye to Kate, she followed Heath out the door.

The temperature was cold, but no wind today. Still, she quickly fished her hat out of a pocket and placed it on her head before shoving her hands into gloves. Short walk or not, she wasn't planning on being frozen to her bones when they arrived.

Heath waited patiently while she finished getting herself together. "You're new to this type of weather, aren't you?" he asked.

Amber liked how it was a question and not a judgement. "Yeah. Where I lived before never got cold like this more than once or twice a winter. Living in subzero temperatures as a daily high has been an education."

He pointed down the street, "We head that way. Place is called 'The Steaming Pot'." They walked quietly for a few moments. "Can I ask where you used to live?"

Amber tensed up for a moment, "Does it matter? This is home now." *Please, let him accept that,* she thought. She wasn't ready to tell him more yet.

"No, it doesn't. You're you, regardless of where you lived before you came here." He paused, "Well, mostly. I mean, if you were some sort of axe murderer and you killed Amanda's real heir and took her place so you could slaughter me. Then I'd want to know."

She glanced up at him, saw the twisted grin on his face as he teased her. "No," she laughed. "Not an axe murderer. Poison is so much more in vogue these days, anyway."

He burst out laughing as she teased him right back.

In a matter of minutes, they arrived at the café. A wealth of aromas assaulted her as Heath opened the door for her to go inside. Coffee, tea, and soup blended perfectly to make for a mouthwatering combination. The eclectic combination of tables and chairs, few matching, welcomed her more than a stuffy, upscale coffee house would've.

"Hey, Heath! How's it going?" a woman called out from behind the counter. Steam rose from the machine in front of her.

"It's going great, Heidi! How's Roy and the kids?" Amber felt him gently push her forward as he responded.

"They're good. Kids can't wait for Thanksgiving break." She wiped her hands on the apron tied around her waist as she met them at the counter. "Don't say anything, but Roy got told he'll be home from Afghanistan before then. We're planning to surprise them at school." The woman's gaze fell on Amber briefly before focusing back on Heath.

"That's great, Heidi. That'll be fun for them."

Heidi's blonde ponytail bobbed as she looked at the pair of them. "So, what can I get you?"

Amber could tell she was curious about who she was, but polite enough not to ask. Larry told her most of the people in Cavendish would wait for her to open up over prying. With the exception of the one cashier, that is. Amber still avoided her when she did her shopping.

"I'm going to go with a breve mocha and some of the chowder today, I think. Amber?" Heath looked at her.

She blinked, and read the neatly lettered chalk board mounted on the wall. "How about a caramel mocha cappuccino and..." she paused. "What's on a Maine Italian?"

Heidi smiled, "Meat, cheese, a few veggies, and a secret sauce that my great-grandma invented."

"Go with that, Amber. You won't regret it." Heath advised.

"Okay, sounds good."

Heidi rang up their order. Amber went to reach for her wallet, but Heath playfully slapped at her hand. "My treat," he insisted as he handed his card over to the blonde woman.

"So, you visiting for long, Amber?" The question was polite as Heidi got started on their drinks.

"Actually, I moved here recently. I'm Amanda Cross' niece."

Heidi's face lit up. "Great! I always loved that old house. Would've been a shame to see it go long without someone living in it." She bent down out of sight, popping up a moment later. "I can't say I met your aunt much. She had a machine at home and didn't care much to sit and chat."

Amber shrugged. "I gotta admit, having the machine at home is nice first thing in the morning. But I've never been one to stay at home all day. I've been working with Kate over at The Cauldron some, simply to get out of the house."

Something shifted on Heidi's face, and some of the friendliness faded. "Well, I suppose that's all well and good. For now, anyway, until you meet more people. We've got an active group at my church, both single and married couples in their twenties. Let me know if you'd like to join us for **Bible** study some night." Heidi set the drinks on the counter and pushed them towards her and Heath.

"Thanks, Heidi," Heath replied for them both. Amber was at a loss. Kate told her the town was open to her being there, having the shop. She didn't know why, but now she was pretty certain Heidi would be happier if Kate closed up and left.

Heath pointed with his free hand toward a small table near a corner. "How's that look?" he asked.

"It's fine," Amber replied. The two moved around a few tables and settled into seats across from each other.

"You'll have to excuse Heidi," Heath said, his voice soft. "Her family's always been religious, not open to anything beyond what they believed. She was worse back in high school, believe it or not. She'd never try to run you out of town, but she'll try to convert you if you give her a chance." He sipped his coffee.

Amber sat back and removed her hat and gloves while she gathered her thoughts. "Where I lived...before...what Kate is, who her shop caters to...it wouldn't have been allowed. The city council was comprised of either church leaders or people active in that community. She wouldn't have been given a permit or business license." She paused, "Kate seems so happy here, so grounded. I'd hate to have someone run her out of town because they don't understand what she truly believes."

"Or what you do?" he asked, giving her a direct look over the rim of his mug.

Amber stared at the light brown liquid in her cup. After the events of the night before, she woke up realizing her Path really was in front of her. No matter what, she'd stay in Cavendish and be Charon's Guardian. If that meant learning more about the Wiccan faith, so be it. She finally felt like she had a purpose to her life, and she clung to it fiercely.

"I can't say I'm there yet, but yeah. It's like I finally found what I've always believed. I just never had a name for it before." She dared to look at him directly. The green eyes that looked back at her were curious, but not judgmental. "Is that a problem for you?" She held her breath. She really liked Heath, but didn't want to start dating him under false pretenses. If his views were the same as Heidi's, better for them both to find out before things moved forward.

Heidi came to the table, setting a steaming bowl in front of Heath and a plate with a sandwich in front of Amber. "I brought over some broth, too," she said as she set a small dish near Amber's sandwich. "Some folks like to dip the sandwich in that. Enjoy!" She moved back to the counter.

Heath reached across the table and placed his hand on top of hers. Amber's stomach tied itself into knots at his touch. "Amber, I like you. A lot. Whatever's in your past, that's for you to tell me when you're ready. Whatever your future may be, well, I just hope you allow me to be part of it."

She looked deep into his green eyes, blown away at the sincerity she saw within them. Maybe one day she could trust him with everything from Texas.

"Amber! There you are!" Larry's voice carried across the café.

Turning around, she saw the lawyer moving quickly over to their table. "Kate told me you'd be here. Mind if I sit down?" he asked as he approached them.

"No, go ahead," she replied. Heath removed his hand from hers and dipped a spoon into his soup. "Is something wrong?"

Larry pulled a chair over from a nearby table and sat down. "I didn't mean to interrupt your lunch. But I told you I'd look into the letter you got a week ago."

She straightened her back, instantly on alert. "Who sent it?" she whispered, trying hard not to let fear creep into her voice.

"Not who you think." She relaxed as he kept talking. "I wasn't able to open it. US Postal regulations say it has to go back to the sender when refused. But I was able to do a search on the return address. Some mailbox store in that town, primarily being used to find graduates from the high school about five years ago. Most likely, a reunion is in the works."

Amber dipped a corner of her sandwich into the juice and took a bite while he explained what he'd found out. "It still doesn't make sense. It's the wrong name. Grace Adams is dead. And how would they find this address?"

"I've got an associate down in Austin. He's a retired Texas Ranger, now freelances as a private detective. If you don't mind, I'd like to give him this information and see if he can find out how the address was discovered, etc. He won't know anything about you. I promise you that. Only that I'm trying to look into a potential mail fraud case.

Because, if someone *else* is using this as a way to find either Grace or you, it's something we need to know."

Amber swallowed, the sandwich settling in her stomach like a lead brick. It could easily be Bruce, using the ruse of a class reunion to find her. But her parents were told never to disclose her address, too.

"If..." She paused, looking for the right words. "If it was one of two individuals who knew where Grace went, what will happen to them?"

Larry gave her hand a reassuring squeeze. "The only thing that would happen is certain things they were given when Grace left would disappear. There would be no harm done to them, unless it was in payment of harm they've done."

Heath cleared his throat, startling her. She'd almost forgotten he was sitting there. "Mr. Dixon, if Amber needs me, I'm in. I don't have a clue what's going on. I don't need to know. But I'm willing to help in whatever way I can to keep her safe."

"Good. You did a great job by being the one who wrote the rejection on the letter. Your handwriting is definitely different than hers." Larry looked at Amber. "If you get any more letters, refuse them outright. And, if Heath's nearby, let him do the scribbling. Don't give whoever's behind this the chance to compare handwriting samples."

She nodded in understanding. "He doesn't believe Grace died, does he?"

"I don't know that yet. I'm going to go call my friend down in Austin and I'll let you know when I have any news." He rose from his seat. "Oh, and Missy wanted me to invite you to our house for Thanksgiving dinner. My wife can be quite adamant, so you've been warned. She's likely to badger you to no end unless you say yes." He smiled at her and glanced at Heath. "You can bring a guest, if you like."

Amber tilted her head at Heath, excited when she saw him do a small nod in acceptance of the unspoken invitation. Looking back at Larry, she said, "I'd like that. Let me know when and where. Oh, and if there's a dress code! I'd hate to show up in jeans and a sweater if everyone else is dressed up!"

Larry smiled, "Will do. I'll let her know to expect you both and call you with details closer to the day." He waved goodbye and left.

Chapter Ten
December

"*H*eath! Where are you taking me?" Amber laughed as he led her blindfolded from the car.

"You'll find out soon enough!" he replied. "No peeking! Okay…watch your step…one up…there you go." Gently he coaxed her out of the vehicle and onto a sidewalk. Or what she thought was one.

The sound of a bell ringing reached her ears, followed by the sound of coins being dropped into a metal container. Several voices called out "Merry Christmas!" and "Happy Holidays!" *Okay…we're downtown somewhere*, she thought. Within three blocks of The Cauldron, most likely. The drive hadn't been long, despite all the turns he made to try and throw her off. There were only three places where donations were being collected by bell ringers. Two were downtown; one was in the cart storage area of the grocery store. Given the stiff wind that assaulted her cheeks, she knew it wasn't the last one.

"Hold on, almost there," he told her, his hand guiding her by her elbow.

"This better be good," she joked. "Or you're going to be in serious trouble!"

"Hold still…right there." He let go of her elbow. Warmth fought against the chill as a blast of aromatic air buffeted her.

He was in front of her now, grabbing both of her hands. "Easy now…you've got two steps to go up. There's the first one," his voice guided her feet as she found the step with the toe of her boot. "That's good. One more, just in front of that one."

She stepped into the warm room and stopped as he let go of her hands. He brushed past her shoulder, closing the door behind him. "Are you ready?" he whispered in her ear.

"Yes!" she laughed. Heath had been hinting for weeks that he was going to take her someplace special tonight. So she wasn't really surprised when he showed up at The Cauldron around closing time. When he insisted on blindfolding her, and Kate encouraged her to play along, that's when she started to wonder just what he was up to.

His fingers began to undo the knot holding the strip of cloth across her eyes. "Close your eyes!" he told her. "No peeking until I tell you!" He removed the cloth.

Still with her eyes closed, Amber called out, "will you please tell me what's going on already?" She heard his feet shuffling as he dashed back around her.

"Okay...on the count of three! One, two, three...surprise!"

Amber's eyes flew open as a group of her friends shouted the last word with him. They stood in Hugo's restaurant, empty but for the small group before her. The chef stood in the center, holding a cake. "Happy birthday and Winter Solstice," they cried out in unison.

She stood there, in shock. No one had ever done much for her birthday before, let alone rented out an entire restaurant to celebrate it as a surprise. "I...um...wow...I can't..." she stammered.

Heath came over and gave her a hug, kissing her on the forehead. "Come on, it's a party!" He led her toward everyone else.

"Blame me, Amber," Larry called out from the back. "Heath was thinking of some nice dinner on the Solstice. When I told him it was your birthday, too, well, it sort of got out of hand."

Still in shock, she looked at him as he stood next to his wife. "I think I forgot," she admitted.

Hugo instantly took command and ordered everyone to find a seat at the table. Within minutes, his wait staff started bringing out dishes full of some of Amber's favorites.

Heath held out a chair for her at the head of the table before taking a seat next to her. Kate and her partner, Jessa, sat opposite of him. Amber hadn't met Jessa often, but knew she treated Kate well. For her, that's all that mattered.

"Why did you do this?" she asked Heath.

He smiled at her, melting her as he did. "Because everyone needs to be celebrated on their birthday, in big ways or small. You've been in Cavendish for just over two months now. I didn't think you knew how much we were all glad for you to be part of our lives now. This seemed to be a good way to show you that we care." He winked, "Though some of us care a bit more than others."

Two hours later, the last of the dishes were removed from the table. Slowly, all of the guests began to filter out the door. "Come on," Heath said as Kate and Jessa left. "I'll give you a ride home. No blindfolds this time, I promise." He smiled.

She gave him a sideways glance. "Is this why you insisted on picking me up to get coffee before work this morning?"

"Guilty as charged," he admitted. "I confess, Your Honor." He waited for her to get her coat, hat, and gloves on before opening the door.

She embraced Hugo near the door, thanking him for the wonderful meal before they left. Following Heath out into the cold night, she slid one of her arms through his.

"If you're in the mood to confess, should I keep interrogating you?"

"You're a heartless wench." He laughed. "Fine. Part of the ride this morning was so I could get you here on time."

"But only part?"

They walked a few more steps, drawing up alongside his car. "If things went well, and you didn't hate me for planning this, then I'd get to have even more time with you on the way home." He reached up and tucked a loose strand of hair back under her hat. "I'm finding it harder and harder to watch you drive off for home." He paused. "I don't want to push you, Amber. If there's stuff from the past you need me to know, you'll tell me when you're ready. I know there's someone out there that you're very afraid of. And that's why you always wanted to drive, to have the escape if you needed it. Tonight, though, I wanted to be the one that left while you watched me drive off."

He went to reach around her and unlock the door. Not sure why, but she leaned in and kissed him gently. He pulled away, his green eyes meeting her brown ones. "Wow," he whispered. "It's your birthday and I'm the one that gets the present."

She felt the blush creep into her cheeks. She bit her lip, unsure how to respond.

He smiled at her and kissed her again, his lips gently brushing against hers. Her knees went weak and her arms snaked around his waist to help her stay on her feet.

"Hey there, you two," Louise's voice called out.

He pulled away from her. Annoyance crossed his features as his head turned toward the voice. Amber lowered her head, allowing the top to rest on Heath's chest. *"Make her go away,"* she whispered.

"Hey, Louise. You're out late tonight," Heath responded.

"I was going to pick up something for dinner from Hugo's, but he seems to be closed. That seems odd, don't you think?" The woman's voice wasn't curious about why the restaurant was closed. Besides, Amber knew Hugo rarely did take-out for anyone beside his favorite people.

"Private party tonight, I think." Heath said. He reached around her and opened the car door behind her. "Amber's not feeling the best, Louise. I'm sure you understand why we won't stay and talk."

Gratefully, Amber slid into the passenger seat and kept her head down. She didn't know why, but she was certain Louise's interest in her wasn't innocent.

"Well, isn't that too bad! Amber, sweetie, can I help?" She all but shoved her way past Heath trying to get to the car.

He shut the door quickly, and Amber saw him put his hands up to stop the other woman from coming too close. Eager to get out of the area, she locked the door and pulled at the seat belt. The uneasy feeling grew.

Heath moved around to the driver's side and got inside. He didn't say a word as he fastened his own seat belt and started the engine. They pulled away from the curb. Amber never bothered to look back.

"That woman gives gossips a good name, I swear," Heath muttered under his breath.

"Is she that bad?"

He flipped on a turn signal and spun the wheel to the right. "By morning, she'll have half of her church group convinced we're all but living together. And the other half will think I'm only after your money."

"Why do people spread rumors like that? It's disgusting!" She slapped at the dashboard in frustration. For the last two months, she thought she'd found someplace that wouldn't be full of lies about her. Dared to believe she'd be allowed to live in peace.

"Because they're mean, unhappy, jealous. Who knows. There's a half dozen reasons. At least most of the town knows where the rumors start. Outside of her little clique, no one's going to believe anything she says."

Amber rested her head in her hand. The edges of a headache began to form in her temple. Tonight was so much fun, and this one woman had tainted it.

They drove in silence the rest of the way to Amber's house. Heath pulled into the driveway and stopped the car. "Wait," he said. Jumping out of the car, he ran around to her side and opened the door. He closed it behind her and walked her to the front door.

"I didn't want to give this to you in the restaurant. Too public," he laughed. "Happy birthday." He placed a small box in her hands. He kissed her once again, turned, and walked back to his car.

She unlocked the door and went inside, locking it again behind her. Minerva came sauntering down the staircase and rubbed against her legs in greeting.

Once she got rid of her coat and everything, she undid the bow around the box. Nestled inside was a charm bracelet with a single heart and a folded piece of paper.

To the woman who has everything, my heart to keep forever ~ Heath

***

The light from the full moon illuminated the black sand beach. The warmth of this reality relaxed her. Her instincts told her that souls would come tonight. The air felt different tonight.

Charon stood in his boat, his hand on the rudder. The first soul arrived, coalescing from a pinpoint of blue light. The child approached Amber, calm. Another soul followed close behind. This was a woman, her features both tired and wary at the same time.

"Charon comes, to ferry the souls," Amber began to speak the ritual words as the woman and child looked at her. The girl smiled at Amber, happily taking the coins from her hand, and skipped toward the boat. The woman, though, hesitated. She kept looking around her, fear in her eyes.

"Have no fear. Pay him at the end and all will be well." Amber tried to calm the woman.

"Bitch!" A man screamed out. Amber turned toward the sound of the voice. Another soul was coming onto the beach.

"Nonononono...." the woman muttered in panic.

Amber spun around and faced her. "Go to the boat, follow the instructions you were given. He cannot harm you again." She spun the woman around and pushed her down the dock to Charon's ferry. "Go. Now."

"Didn't I tell you that I'd follow you wherever you went, bitch!" the man screamed as he strode toward the dock. "Don't you dare get into the boat, you whore! I own your soul!"

Amber stepped in front of him. "Charon comes, to ferry the souls."

His angry face focused on her. "Get out of my way, bitch. None of you are good for anything but whoring!" He raised a hand, ready to strike her.

She stared him down and kept speaking. "The Ferryman knows the sum of your life."

He met her gaze, hatred and loathing seething under his skin. He was almost on the dock, would soon be solid. She held her head high and met his gaze defiantly. "Take this coin, pay him when you arrive." She held out two coins.

"I don't have to pay him nothin', bitch!" He slapped the coins from her hand.

"Then let your doom be pronounced," she intoned. It was the last thing she'd learned from the book. How to end the ritual if a soul refused the coin.

The pentacle Amber had left her began to glow and a warmth flooded through her body. Shock registered on the face of the man as she transformed. Into what, she didn't know. The illusion would be different for each soul. She became the one thing they truly feared.

In panic, he ran into the river and tried to climb into the boat. Pale arms began to reach up from the water and pulled at his body, dragging him underneath to his final punishment. The aura surrounding her faded along with his screams.

Charon looked at her, nodded once, and began to maneuver his boat away from the dock. There would be no more souls coming this night.

Chapter Eleven
January

*A*mber sat on the dock, her back against one of the support pillars. "What's it like, Charon?"

The Ferryman looked at her, "What's what like?"

"Ferrying souls. Being judge and jury and executioner?"

"Ah, that. It's what I do. What I was created to do. I can't say there's a way to describe it that you'd understand."

This was the third full moon since Amanda left. No souls had come this time, so Amber took the opportunity to try and find out more of this being she was supposed to guard.

She looked back toward the house. He normally didn't stay this long. "Does it bother you, knowing you have to do what you do to some of them?"

"No. I have no emotions. My position doesn't allow for those. The souls who go to torment have earned that fate as much as those who are blessed with a more pleasant afterlife."

She started, looking back at him. "You don't feel anything, then? Not even love? Compassion?"

He shrugged. "I am loyal only to my Guardians. They keep the souls who are still alive from crossing before their time. Keep my existence a secret." He paused. "Amanda and I talked often. She would tell me what was happening in your world. The awake world. How many were being killed or told they weren't even truly human simply because of faith or something stupid like that. There were those who lived and preached I was a demon and should be hunted down. I am grateful for you and the rest who risk so much to make sure those who believe can safely go to their final rest. For that reason, I will defend you in any way I can."

She put her feet under her and rose. "I appreciate that."

It had been quiet since November. Larry's detective friend was still looking around, but was trying hard not to rouse suspicion. She and Heath were dating, yes. The pace was slow. She was still afraid of shadows from her past, but he wasn't pushing it. Louise even backed down. Jessa exploded in the grocery store one day, when Louise ran her mouth about Kate "cheating" on her with Amber. She'd kept her distance from Amber and Heath after that, as well as Kate and Jessa. For almost two months now.

Between the library at home and the one at The Cauldron, she'd learned so much about Wicca. Enough that she now openly wore the pentacle Amanda had left her. She'd worn it initially on the full moon, to guide the souls. Now it was as common to her as the bracelet from Heath.

"Do you dance, Amber?" Charon's voice cut through her reverie.

"Not really, why?"

He reached down and pulled a small harp out from under one of the seats. "I was going to play something tonight. Imbolic is nearing. The snow you've lived with will begin to melt soon. Is that not worth celebrating?" His fingers began to pluck and strum the strings on the instrument.

Amber closed her eyes, letting the music embrace her. There was something joyful in the notes, hopeful. She began to dance.

Her body swayed with the music, her feet finding steps she didn't know she knew. Somehow, she ended up on the beach. Her toes kissed the edge of the water as she gave herself over to the magic Charon's music woke in her.

It wasn't until the last notes faded away that she realized how free she felt.

She looked at him, her chest heaving from the exertion. She couldn't find words to explain the simple yet profound joy she felt.

"Time for me to move on. Until next month, Guardian." He maneuvered the craft away from the dock and disappeared into the mist.

Amber walked back into the house, locking the door behind her. She replaced the pouch in the fireplace and headed upstairs to bed.

***

"*L*ater, guys!" Doug called out to his friends. Louise relaxed a little. She didn't mind when poker night was at their house most nights. Tonight, though, she'd been bored. The snow was deep this year, and she hadn't felt like visiting with some of her friends while her husband's friends took over the table for poker night.

She absently clicked through some of her favorite entertainment gossip sites on her computer. One year, she'd convince Doug to go to Florida for the winter. Or a Caribbean cruise. Anything to break up the monotony of Cavendish in the winter!

January was the worst. No more holiday lights, turkeys, or colorful costumes. Oh, sure, Valentine's Day was not far off. But she and Doug had been married for over forty years. Their kids were long grown and gone, raising their own families.

So, she sat at her computer and dreamed of a life outside of the snowbound town she lived in. Where everyone was beautiful, thin, rich. The sun always bright enough to wear sunglasses, even at a memorial service.

Wait...what? She thought, her hand maneuvering the mouse to click back a page. The photo in the corner of a sobbing man coming out of a whitewashed church in some small town in Texas moved her. She clicked on the link and her hand flew to her mouth in shock as she read the article. *The poor man, how sad! To lose his fiancée in such a tragic way!*

She scrolled down a bit further to see a photo of the girl so tragically lost at sea after a kidnapping. "Doug!" she screamed. "Come here!"

"What's wrong?" he asked, darting into the room.

Louise pointed at her screen, her finger shaking violently. "Look at this photo! It's Amber Cross! I know it!" She scooted her chair back so Doug could get a closer look. "The poor boy! To think she was dead all this time when she's here living under an assumed name!"

Doug deftly moved the mouse and closed down the browser. "Enough, Louise. No conspiracies of yours this time. Leave Ms. Cross alone."

Louise sputtered. "But...that boy was her fiancée! And who knows what happened to the real Amber! She's probably at the bottom of the Atlantic! He has a right to know she's alive and living here under an assumed name!"

He held up a hand, halting her in the middle of her excited ranting. "No, Louise. Larry's the one that brought Amber here. She is who she says she is, end of statement. Unless you think Larry's capable of committing fraud?" She shook her head slowly. "Good. Now, put this out of your head and come to bed. Whoever that boy lost is gone for good. I don't want to hear another word about it."

Louise watched Doug leave the room and spun back to the computer. Quickly, she reopened the browser and found the last page, bookmarking it in a file she knew Doug would never look at.

"Louise, come to bed!" he called out.

"Coming, sweetie!" she replied. She had tomorrow off at the store. Doug would be at his job all day. She could investigate more later.

Chapter Twelve
February

"*I*f Wiccans don't celebrate Valentine's Day, why all the hearts?" Amber asked as she helped Kate move decorations around the shop.

"Because," she replied as she removed a string of small pink heart shaped lights from a nail high up on the wall, "love is universal. It's not just on a single day each year, or dependent on a saint from another faith to determine what's right and not. Love is love. There's more forms of that than hate, which is why it's more powerful." She wound up the last cord and handed it to Amber. "That should be the last string. Good thing we checked for burned out bulbs before we took them down."

Placing the strand into the storage box, Amber straightened up. "Yeah. I'd hate to put them up next year and find them dead."

"Happens every year," Kate laughed. "There's always going to be one or two out before the holiday hits."

Amber played with a Tibetan singing bowl near the register. "So, when are you asking Jessa?"

"That, my friend, is not a detail I care to share with you," she laughed. "It'll happen when it happens. We've been together for over five years now. The commitment is there. The legal stuff will follow when it's time."

Amber smiled and started to help Kate get the boxes put back in the right spot in the storeroom. She knew Kate was right. That's one of the biggest things she'd learned from her studies. Things happen when they're supposed to happen. Easier to let life flow than to fight against it.

Stretching upward on her toes, she slid one of the boxes into place just as the bell rang, alerting them both to a customer. "I've got it," Kate said as she darted through the beaded curtain.

"Amber, come out here. Please." Kate's voice was calm, serious. Something wasn't right.

Cautiously, she moved aside the curtain. The beads rustled against each other. Heath and Larry both stood in the shop. Along with another gentleman. And a cop.

"Amber, we have a situation," Larry kept his voice low.

Desperate to quell the fear rising in her, she took a few deep breaths and tried to find her center. "What's wrong?" she whispered.

"Kate, is there someplace we can talk privately?" The officer spoke up. "This isn't something we need the entire town to know about."

"Hold on." Her friend dashed to the front door. Flipping the sign to "closed," she threw the deadbolt. "There. I've closed randomly before. No one will notice a problem. There's a side room here." She gestured past a small archway. "No windows to the outside for anyone to see us together."

Larry gestured for Amber and Kate to lead the way. Something was wrong, no doubt about it.

The small room was where Kate would do an occasional reading. For the most part, though, it was a library and classroom. Comfortable chairs and cushions were intermixed with bookshelves and small tables.

Amber slid into one of the chairs. Kate took one next to her. Heath reached out and snagged a beanbag chair, pulling it closer before lowering himself into it.

"Amber, I don't want to alarm you," Larry began.

"Too bad, because you already have. What's going on, Larry?"

"This is John Taylor. He's our local sheriff. Before you get scared, he knew about everything before I left to get you. Before Amanda died."

She turned her focus to the sheriff. "You've known this whole time?"

The man nodded, "Amanda took me into her confidence a few weeks before she died. Had me witness her final draft of her will. She knew your ex-boyfriend wouldn't take your departure well, and wanted to make sure I knew the circumstances, all of them, before you arrived. Your safety was her biggest concern. Given Bruce's position and family connections, it was for the best."

"What do you mean?"

"He made some inquiries, sent out some APBs, shortly after you disappeared. Somehow, he found out where your aunt was from. He was coming up with all sorts of reasons why we should apprehend you, all very unfounded. I simply ignored his demands for 'proof' you weren't here and told him that no one fitting that description had moved to Cavendish recently."

"Something's changed, though. Hasn't it?" She felt Heath's hand encompass hers. She hadn't told him anything about her past, but still he was there to support her.

"I'll let Doug fill you in on that." Officer Taylor moved aside, allowing the other man to come forward.

"Louise is my wife, Amber. And she's not perfect. Not by a long shot. I've known for some time now that she's been meddling with people in town, starting rumors or such. But it's been harmless so far. The town knows she's a gossip and tends to ignore her. Even when Jessa launched into her the other day." He coughed and glanced at Kate. "I apologize for that, Kate. Louise had absolutely no business trying to infer you and Amber were having an affair. She's still bitter that you beat our granddaughter at the state tennis tournament back in high school."

Kate nodded silently.

He looked back at Amber. "A couple of weeks ago, right after poker night at our house, she called me to her computer in a panic. She'd found some article about a grieving family in Texas. Seems a young woman, about your age, was kidnapped and then lost at sea in a plane crash. The article included a photo of the girl. Louise was certain it was you."

"Lord and Lady…" Kate swore under her breath.

Doug took a breath before continuing. "I told her to leave it alone, that the girl in the photo was dead and gone."

"But she didn't, did she?" Amber asked.

"No. I got a call this morning from the manager of the grocery store. Seems Louise was found in the security office when he came to work. She'd somehow made herself a key. And she was pulling footage of you in the store to add to an email."

Larry spoke up, "Amber, she hit send on that e-mail before her manager stopped her."

"She sent it to Bruce." She didn't even make it a question. Her voice, flat and even, sounded dead to her own ears. She knew the answer without any confirmation.

Doug turned back to the sheriff. "John, do me a favor. Keep Louise in jail for a few days. It's Friday. I need to think about some things. I don't plan to bail her out right away." He turned his attention back to her. "As soon as I got the call, I contacted Larry. He told me about your past, Amber. Louise really took things too far this time. If there's anything I can do to make up for this, just tell me."

"Right now, her security is paramount." Larry interjected. "It's not going to be long before Bruce shows up. Probably armed. He's got every right to carry his firearm, even on a plane. And I have no doubt he'll be here as soon as he can."

"I'm working some of that already," Officer Taylor responded. "I have a few friends in the TSA in Bangor. They'll find reasons to delay him when he lands, give me a call when he's left the airport. I'm also going to station an officer outside your home and here at the shop. We're not going to be far away."

"That's fine outside, but what if he breaks into her house when she's here and waits for her?" Heath spoke up. "I'm not sure you should even go back home until we find him, Amber."

Amber glanced at a calendar on the wall. The full moon was tomorrow night. "I have to be home, Heath. I can't stay somewhere else." She kept her voice firm. "Don't argue with me on this. There's something I have to take care of there."

"Amber, Minerva will be fine—"

"It's not about Minerva, Heath. I can't explain it right now, but I have to be home at night."

"I can keep an eye on things here at the shop. She can work in the back. That door doesn't open from the outside anyway. And Jessa and I can make sure things are clear before she comes in each day." Kate spoke up.

"Okay, then I'm staying at the house with you each night, Amber." Heath responded.

She looked at him, her head tilted to one side. "I don't need you to move in with me! I can take care of myself!"

He smiled, "I know you can. Let's just say I want to make sure I have a bowl of popcorn ready while I watch you kick this Bruce guy's ass."

Larry said, "I like that idea, Heath. That settles it. John, let me know the minute you hear he's in the state and we'll ramp up security around The River House. I've got a friend whose been keeping an eye on things down in Texas for me for a couple of months already, so we'll get some warning that he's on the way. Until then—" he pointed at Amber, "—you don't go anywhere alone. You stick with Kate or Heath, you hear me? I'll get in touch with Ms. Cole, see if she can get here in time. She'll shadow you and you'll never even know she's there." His face softened as he looked at her. "Amanda would come back and haunt my dreams if I let Bruce get his hands on you again, Amber. We're going to keep you safe. Have no fear."

Much as she wanted to believe him, her stomach still roiled. Fear was trying hard to win over the confidence she'd gained.

"C'mon, Amber," Heath rose and held a hand out to her. "Let's get something to eat. You need to do something normal right now. He's not going to show up for at least several hours. No need to jump at shadows yet."

Kate nudged her back, "He's right, Amber. Go. Eat something. Try to laugh. You're in for a rough few days, but we had warning." She looked up at Doug, "Thank you for that. You may have saved her life today."

"Least I could do, after what Louise's meddling has cost you and many others in this town." He shook Larry's hand, and then Officer Taylor's. "Amber, I hope we catch this guy. Before he can hurt you. Don't give Louise a thought. She's where she needs to be. It might even be the one thing that gets her to stop pulling this crap." He started to leave, then paused and turned back around. "Kate, can you let me back out? I'm not sure you're ready to open up again."

She rose, giving Amber a reassuring pat on her shoulder as she did. "Sure, Doug."

"We're heading out, too," Amber said as Kate left the room. "I just have to grab a few things from the back."

She started for the storeroom, knowing Heath followed close behind her. "If he's not here yet, there's no reason for you to ghost me," she chided him.

"I already explained that, Amber. I'm going to make sure you're well stocked on popcorn before you go home tonight."

She laughed as she pushed aside the curtain. Flipping on the light, she threw on her coat. "Where did you want to get lunch?" she asked.

"Dunno. Want to go back over to 'The Steaming Pot' or hike a few blocks over to grab some pizza?"

"Pizza sounds yummy!" She put her hat on her head and grabbed her purse, slinging it over her shoulder. "I'd just as soon drive, though. Meet you there?"

She saw the hesitation cross his face, "Heath, you heard everyone just now. It's at least a four-hour flight from Texas to Bangor, plus the drive here. It'll take this guy even longer given that the only flights out of Louden are puddle hoppers to Dallas or San Antonio. He's got to leave town to even get here."

"Louden, Texas? That's where you're from?" He kept his voice soft.

"Yeah. But it's not where I belong. Not then, not now."

He leaned in closer to her, one arm circling her waist. "Where do you belong, then?"

She smiled. "I'm really thinking upstate Maine is a good place to stay."

"Good," he whispered. "I'd hate to love a Texas gal who only wanted to go back there instead of stay here." His head bent, softly kissing her on the lips.

Yeah, she thought. *I'd hate to love a Maine guy and not stay, too.*

Chapter Thirteen

They met up at the pizza place and found a table. Amber looked around as Heath went to place the order. Somehow, she'd never realized how close this restaurant was to the police station. Knowing Louise was sitting in there, behind bars, made her feel safer somehow.

Her phone beeped. She picked it up off the table and read the text from Larry:

Confirmed he left for Dallas an hour ago. From there, he goes to DC before connecting flight to Bangor. Heavy snow expected there before they arrive, so he'll have to cool his heels for a while. Weather's giving us almost a full day to prepare.

She replied that she understood, placing the phone back down just as Heath approached the table with their drinks.

"Everything okay?" he asked as he put the tray down.

She grabbed one of the glasses of soda and nodded. "Yeah. Bruce is in the air already, but there's a big storm heading to DC. He'll have to wait out the time at the airport. Larry doesn't think he'll be here now until sometime tomorrow afternoon or evening at the earliest."

"Is Larry going to have you leave town?"

"I can't, Heath. I have to be home tomorrow night. I can't explain it," she reached across the table and grabbed his hand. "There's something I have to do, something I don't dare miss."

"Amber, I get that. I really do. Even if I don't know what it is, I can see it's important to you. But your life is important to me. Can't you put it off a few days?"

"No, I can't. And I wouldn't even if I could." She paused, swirling the straw around in her glass. Looking up at him, she said, "I can't run from this forever, Heath. I know that now. When I came here, yes. I was running from Bruce. From everything that happened in Texas. But now...how do I say this...it's like that life wasn't the one I was meant to have. This one is, here in Cavendish. With you, Kate, Minerva, The River House, all of it. This is my life. It's the Path I've always supposed to be on. I'm more Amber Cross now than I ever was the person Bruce knew." She paused again, trying to put everything she felt into words and not sure how. "It's like that life was a nightmare and I've finally woken up from it. I know who I am now, who I will be in the future. And that person will never be controlled by another. My future is up to me."

He looked down, one finger playing with the charm on the bracelet he'd given her for her birthday. "Am I part of that future?"

"Yes, if you want to be."

"Does that mean I'll eventually know the whole story?" She felt her body stiffen at his question. "I don't mean now." The words rushed from his mouth. "When you're ready to tell it to me. I don't know who this Bruce guy is, other than some ex of yours from Texas. But I can tell he hurt you deeply. For that reason only, I'd risk everything to keep you from having to see him again. Eventually, though, I'd like to know the whole story. What life was like then, why you have to stay home tomorrow."

She smiled. "Maybe one day. I'm not going to run from him any longer. If he's coming here, he's going to find I'm not the same person he remembers. That alone might be enough to scare him away."

The waiter brought the pizza over to them, and they kept the conversation light as they ate. A thought entered Amber's mind as Heath got up to get a box for them to take the leftovers back home. By the time he came back and they were ready to go, she knew what she had to do next.

They walked out into the cold again. "Heath," she said as she stood near her SUV, "I'm not going right home. You can head there, or run home if you need to. But there's something over there—" she nodded at the police station, "—that I have to do."

"I'd rather not leave you alone if I can help it, Amber. I know he's not here yet, but I'm nervous about the whole situation. I can go do that with you, then we can run past my place before we head to yours."

She smiled at him, "Okay. Grab your popcorn. This should be interesting to watch." She darted across the street towards the police station. No reason to move her car a block.

Walking into the station, she approached the front desk. "I understand Louise Dumont was arrested earlier today. Is it possible for me to see her?"

The desk attendant handed her a clipboard, "Sign in here. You have to leave your purse, keys, and cell phone here." She pointed at a bank of lockers lining the side wall. "Go ahead and lock it all up and then hand me the key."

Amber nodded her understanding and did as she was instructed. Heath threw his wallet, keys, and phone in the same locker. Securing it, she handed the key over to the clerk.

Another officer waited on the other side of a metal detector. They walked through and then he escorted them through a secure door.

It wasn't a big facility, and it was a short walk back to the holding cells. "You guys want to talk to her privately, or what?"

"You don't have to move her, if that's what you mean. What I have to say won't matter to anyone besides her and me," Amber assured him.

The officer shrugged and led them to another door. "This is the holding cell area. It's slow right now. No one's stupid enough to get drunk when there's more than a foot of snow on the ground. They'll freeze to death before we find them. She's the only one in there." He swiped his card through an ID reader. The mechanism began to turn, echoing in the quiet corridor. "Don't approach the cell, though. No passing anything to her. Stay against the wall. I'll be watching the monitor"—he motioned to a small desk with a video feed on top—"so just wave when you're ready to leave."

The door clicked open and he swung it open, allowing her and Heath to enter.

The stark white of the room made the dull gray bars stand out. A wooden bench, bolted to the wall, sat directly opposite of the cell. "I'll be here if you need me," Heath whispered as he moved to sit down.

Amber nodded once, then turned her attention to the lone occupant in the cell.

Louise sat on a bunk, her normally neat hair disheveled. Redness ringed her eyes. She'd been crying. *More because she felt she was being treated unjustly than any remorse over what she'd done*, Amber thought.

"What are you doing here?" Louise asked.

Amber shrugged, "I had to see the woman who chose to try and destroy my life. And didn't succeed."

Louise stood up, moving closer to the bars. "You deserved it. That poor boy! Your parents! How could you do that to them! What about the 'real' Amber Cross? Is she the one at the bottom of the Atlantic?"

Smiling, Amber snorted. "Really? You're that bored with your own life that you have to invent stories about those around you? If you were tired of your life, just move. Divorce Doug, whatever. But to try and destroy the lives of people through innuendo and half-truths? You're truly a pitiful excuse for a person.

"For your information, Bruce and I were never engaged." She stared Louise down, daring her to break off for her gaze. "We dated, once. In high school. He beat me, tried to rape me. I fought back and ran. My parents thought he was perfect, never understood why I wouldn't see him after that night. I thought I was free when he went to college. Only he came back. Got a job with the police department. Told anyone that would listen that we were engaged. But we weren't.

"He spent the last two years systematically stalking me. He got me fired from countless jobs so I'd have no way to support myself. No way to save up for a car or any other way to leave town. My parents believed his lies, kept asking me to set a date for the wedding. That's when Larry came to see me.

"I AM Amanda Cross' legal heir. It was at her urging that I changed my name. There was no one on board the plane when it went into the ocean. We left all traces of my old life on there to try and convince Bruce the woman he knew, Grace Adams, was dead. I became Amber Cross willingly. The name was of my own choosing. Everything was perfectly legal. I did this to escape a boy who was intent on possessing me, abusing me. Simply because I was the only woman in his life that ever told him no."

She watched Louise's face grow pale and her body wince with her words. "And, now, because of you, I'm having to fight him again. I have to deny him from destroying my very soul simply because he can't handle someone who is stronger than he is. This is the harm you have caused by trying to be 'nice' to the 'poor boy'. If any harm comes to me, Heath, Kate, Larry, or anyone I care for because of Bruce, it's on you. And I will make sure you are held accountable."

"But…but…I didn't know!" Louise whimpered.

Amber snorted. "You do now. Good-bye, Louise. Unless I'm called to testify against you, which I would have no problem doing, I have no intention on seeing you again. Or thinking of you. I have to take care of the consequences of your actions. But I don't have to consider your feelings in the process."

She turned, giving a thumb's up at the camera in the corner. Heath rose to join her. Without another look at the woman who tried to ruin her life, she left.

She didn't bother to make sure Heath was with her. She'd said more than she originally intended, but that was fine. Louise now knew how much her meddling had cost, knew that Amber wouldn't be afraid to testify against her.

As to Heath, well, he knew about all there was to know about her now. Either he'd run for the hills or stay by her side. Sure, she had a preference. But it was his choice, not hers.

She was long done with the idea of forcing someone to love another. If nothing else, Bruce taught her how bad that was.

Reclaiming her locker key, she handed Heath his possessions before retrieving her own items. She nodded once in thanks to the officer behind the desk and walked through the door as Heath held it open for her.

They didn't speak during the short walk back to the cars. She stood by her door, and took a deep breath. "Well, now you know…stuff. Still plan to be my watchdog for the next day or two?"

He pulled her into his arms. Melting against his chest, she finally relaxed and let go of a long breath. "To me, you're Amber. This Grace person is someone else, someone that doesn't matter to me. Bruce needs to pay what he did to her. And I will do whatever I can to make sure any lingering residue of crap he put the woman I love through is dealt with. Even if that means I end up in a cell next to Louise."

She pulled away from him, but left her arms circling his waist. "Don't worry. You won't. I know someone else who can make sure there's nothing left of Bruce for anyone to find."

He smiled. "Really? Got mob connections, too?"

Laughing, she let go and found the key to her door. "No, not quite. But he certainly knows how to get rid of bodies." She turned away, unlocking the driver's side. "Let's go to your place, get what you need for a day or two. If Bruce is coming to find Grace, I want to make sure things are ready for him to think twice before becoming…insistent."

"That's a new word for it," Heath shrugged. "I figured we'd have to all but kill him and then hand him over to Sheriff Taylor and Larry so the legal system could deal with him."

"Words have power, Heath. More than you can imagine. I really don't wish him ill. I simply want him to leave me in peace." She got into her SUV. "I'll follow you to your place, then we'll head out to The River House. Minerva's probably wondering why I'm not home to feed her." She shut the door and buckled her seat belt as she watched him walk over to his car.

While he ran inside his house to get what he needed, she listened to the weather forecast, trying to get a feel for how bad the storm bearing down on D.C. was. Knowing Bruce as she did, she wouldn't be surprised if he rented a car over cooling his heels at the airport. She grabbed her phone and sent a quick text to Larry with the idea. The roads would be even worse, if flights were grounded. No matter what, he'd be in Cavendish before midnight. Which meant she'd have to deal with him before or during her time as Charon's Guardian.

Fifteen minutes later, both vehicles were safely sheltered in the carriage house and she led Heath through the sheltered tunnel to the house. "Minerva!" she called out as she put her coat and scarf on a hook near the back door. "I'm home."

Sliding past Heath, she said, "Go ahead and put your coat on a peg. Kitchen's just around the corner to your right if you want to get the pizza in the fridge." She twisted the dead bolt and regular lock, then also slid on the chain and gate latch at the top of the frame.

"Meow," Minerva complained, rubbing against Amber's legs.

"I know, it's ten minutes past your dinner time," she laughed. She scooped up the empty dish on the floor. "Heath, can you grab me a can of cat food from the pantry?" she asked. Placing the dish on the counter, she pulled open a drawer and grabbed a spoon.

"Sure," he said. He opened a few cupboards before locating the correct one. "Here you go," he said as he slid a can across the counter toward Amber.

Minerva continued to both complain and rub against Amber as she popped the lid and scooped the contents out into the dish. Kneeling down, she put the dish on the ground in front of the cat. Minerva dove into her meal.

Laughing, she muttered, "Pushy," as she straightened. She tossed the spoon into the sink.

"Where can I stash my stuff?" Heath asked.

"I'll show you," she replied as she dropped the empty can into a recycling bin near the back door. "There's lots of room upstairs. Unless you really like sleeping on the couch."

"No, not since college," he laughed.

She flipped on the hall switch, illuminating the staircase. "Surprised you don't know where more things are around here. I thought Amanda had you over a lot to fix things." She started up the staircase.

"Most of what I saw of the house was outside or the basement. She hired a contractor from out of town for the major renovation, one that specialized in historical homes. I pretty much dealt with the hot water heater, furnace, that sort of stuff. Small stuff that she didn't need a big team to handle."

She rounded the corner at the top of the stairs. "Left side's all guest rooms and a bathroom. Right side's my rooms."

"Rooms? Please tell me you don't have a closet dedicated to nothing but shoes!" He laughed.

"Nah, it's how Amanda set it up. Private bed and bath, pass through closet, office, that sort of thing." She leaned against a wall closest to her bedroom door as he opened the door opposite hers.

Something stirred within her. She knew she loved him, had all but told him. And he'd been so good at letting her pace how their relationship progressed. The one time she'd come close to being intimate with someone was the night Bruce tried to force himself on her. She knew, however, it could be, it would be, totally different with Heath.

She watched him survey the room through the open door. The sports bag he'd brought sat on the bed. The room was neutral. She'd not taken the time to add any of her personality to it yet.

He turned, a puzzled look crossing his face, and walked back to her. "Everything okay?" he asked. "I've never seen that look on your face before. I can't tell if you're happy or scared."

"A little bit of both, to be honest. There's something I want, but it's not an easy thing to ask for."

He reached out and stroked her cheek. "You won't know until you ask, though. Am I right?"

She moved closer to him, kissing him deeply. All of her desire for him, and fear, flowed into the kiss. After a minute, she pulled away from him and whispered, "You heard what he tried to do to me. I'd like to have a better memory of being intimate with someone than that."

He gently grasped each side of her head, staring at her. "If that's what the woman I love needs, that's what she'll get." He kissed her, and she responded with her own passion.

Her hand felt for the doorknob to her bedroom. Twisting it, she flung the door open. "Make sure it stays open," she breathed heavily as his lips moved to her neck. "Minerva raises a fuss if she can't get in when I'm in here."

She felt him scoop her up into his arms and lay her on the massive bed. And no longer cared if Minerva was in the room or not.

Chapter Fourteen

*W*hen she woke up, she was alone in the bed. The covers next to her were pulled aside. He was awake already.

The smell of fresh brewed coffee began to tease her nose. Throwing on a thick robe, she belted it closed and began to make her way downstairs.

She met him on the landing, a tray filled with food in his hands. His bare chest made her blush slightly, remembering how good it felt to explore it the night before.

"Back to bed with you!" he teased. "How am I supposed to surprise you with this,"— he raised the tray— "if you're not in bed?"

She stared at the tray, amazed. "No one's ever brought me breakfast in bed before."

"Good. I'm the first! Now, back to bed with you!" He used the tray to motion her back to the room.

Laughing, she darted up the stairs and back down the hall to her room. She dove back into the bed and drew the covers over her lap as he came in with the tray.

"Surprise!" he called.

"Wow," she said, feigning a yawn. "I had no idea!"

He slid the tray over her lap as they both laughed. Maneuvering past the bench at the end, Heath climbed in next to her. "Hope you like omelets," he said. "I'm no good with pancakes and couldn't find a waffle iron." He slid one of the plates off and onto his own lap.

Amber took a sip of coffee from one of the steaming mugs. "No, this is perfect! I love it!"

They ate in silence for a few moments. "You really never had anyone bring you breakfast in bed before?" Heath asked. "Not even your mom when you were sick as a kid?"

Amber shook her head. "Nope. She was certain that I'd make a mess and spill everything, which meant she'd have to clean it up."

"Well," he said between bites, "I'm glad to end that streak. You'll have to give me a list of all the things you always wanted to do and haven't. Then I know what I need to do to really surprise you."

She nuzzled his neck, whispering, "Last night was certainly on that list. And it was amazing."

"Amazing, huh?" He moved his plate back onto the tray and placed it on the bench. Crawling back over the bed, he grinned at her. "Maybe this morning I should try for awesome or earth shattering." He began to kiss the base of her throat through her robe.

Leaning against the headboard, Amber let the emotions wash over her, feeling her skin tingle and erupt in fire as he kissed her.

Her phone, charging on the nightstand, buzzed loudly. Heath stopped as Amber glanced at it. "It's Larry," she said as she reached for the phone.

"Amber, everything okay?" Larry's voice came across the phone as she answered it.

"Yeah, I'm fine. Heath and I were just eating breakfast. What's up?"

"Got a call just now. Rental car agencies in D.C. all shut down because of the storm, so Bruce is still cooling his heels at Dulles. My contact said the crews were working on getting flights going again, though, so I think we've got about twelve hours, maybe fourteen, before he hits Cavendish."

"What about Ms. Cole? Were you able to find her?" Heath gently rubbed her shoulders as she spoke.

"She's out of the country dealing with a personal matter. It'll be the officers Sheriff Taylor can spare, but we won't have her help in keeping him away."

Amber took a deep breath. "It's okay. I'm hoping he gives up and goes away. No one says I have to answer the door when he knocks."

"You staying home today, then? I know we've got some more time, but this whole situation has me nervous. I'd feel better if you left town. Amanda would have my hide if I let anything happen to you."

She glanced over at Heath as he lounged on the bed next to her. The idea of spending the entire day with him, either in or out of bed, appealed to her. "I'll be fine. I'm sure Heath and I will find something to do around here."

"I heard about your visit to Louise yesterday, by the way."

"I needed to make sure she understood the price her meddling cost, that's all."

"She understands it now, that's for certain. She tried to get me to represent her, but I declined. Even after she said she wasn't planning on fighting any charges the D. A. brought against her."

Amber sighed, "Maybe she'll learn. Maybe she won't. It's not up to me to force her either way."

"No, it's not. I need to go. I'll call Sheriff Taylor, let him know you're staying put today. He'll make sure the house is watched until Bruce is heading back to Texas. I'll call again when we know he's on the road here." Larry hung up.

Amber placed the phone back on the table, unsure of how she felt. She wasn't afraid of what was coming now. Bruce no longer terrified her. Waiting for him to show up, though, made her stomach churn.

"So, what was so important that you had to stay here today?" Heath asked.

She looked over at him, lounging on the bed. One hand was cradling his head as the other absently caressed the bare leg that protruded from her bathrobe.

She tossed her head back against the headboard. "It won't happen for hours yet. Not until midnight. And, to be honest, I have no clue if you'll be allowed to witness it." Amber looked down at him. His eyes stared at her, intent on every word. "But something happens at this house on the full moon. It's why Amanda chose me. Somehow, she knew I'd be able to fulfill the role."

Heath's face creased in thought. "Every full moon? Huh. I never made that connection before, but I remember Amanda always being home then. And she never wanted anyone on the property at night. If she threw a party, everyone had to be gone before eleven."

She kept watching him, waiting for him to continue. He wasn't dumb, but she wanted to find out what he thought went on before really telling him more.

"Why wouldn't I be able to see what happens?" he asked.

Leaning forward, her hands nervously picked at some of Minerva's cat hairs that decorated the bed. "Things out back...change. There's always been a Wiccan living here, even when practicing in public meant death. Their job is to guard what comes on the full moon, to guide those who would meet them. I know you're okay with my faith, but I don't know yours. It may prevent you or Bruce from seeing what I do." She tried to keep it vague, but felt like she was falling short.

"So, you're a guardian or a guide or something like that?"

Amber nodded.

Heath rolled over onto his stomach and pushed himself up on his arms and straddled her. "Does that mean I'm the guardian of the Guardian?" he smirked.

"Tonight, very possibly. I don't know what he's going to do, or if either of you will witness what I do. All I know is that, should Bruce go outside after me, it will not end well."

119

"For you, or for him?"

She met his gaze. "Him."

Heath sat back, "You're trying to protect him? What happens, Amber? I really don't want to pry, but if him following you out there will make him get out of your life for good, why not let it happen?" Confusion and anger tainted his voice.

She drew her knees up under her chin. "It goes against the Rede. It's doing harm. If he goes out there of his volition, the doom is on him. If I trick him in some way, it comes back on me." She reached a hand out and took his. "I want him gone. But what would happen to him...I wouldn't wish that on anyone. If he does it to himself, fine. But I have to try and prevent him from doing it."

"What happens, Amber? I need to know. If I'm going to try and stop him, I need to know why."

"This isn't just a house that's got a river in the back yard, Heath. On a full moon, the grass becomes a black sand beach. The river moves closer. The water becomes thick, black. So dark that the moonlight can't pierce the surface. There's a wooden dock. And that's where the Ferryman secures his boat."

Heath's eyes flew open. "You're talking about a myth, Amber."

"It's not a myth, Heath. It's real. The River Styx flows behind this house on the full moon. Charon arrives and ferries the souls of the dead. I'm the current Guardian. I give coins and instructions to those who come to this waystation to ride his ferry."

He fell back, his hands flying to his face as he tried to absorb what she'd told him.

"And, if Bruce goes out there?"

"Charon protects me as much as I protect him. Should Bruce go on the ferry and refuse my instruction...should he pay him before he gets off..." her voice trailed off. The screams of the man as the river itself dragged him under the surface still haunted her months later.

"That's why all the mythology warned people not to pay the Ferryman."

"If he gives him coins before he gets off, or refuses to take what I hand him, his fate is sealed. Charon will make the final judgement on his soul."

Heath let out a huge breath. "Wow. I mean, it doesn't change anything for me. I'm going to do whatever I can to keep Bruce from getting to you. But now I understand why you can't just let him go back without warning. And why Amanda never let the parties go that late."

"You'll stay, then? Knowing what it is I do here?"

He sat back up and held up a single finger. "One condition. Not all at once, not now. But sometime between now and next month's full moon, you tell me about Texas. Why you left, why you chose the name of Amber Cross. And what you hated so much about that life."

She smiled. "Agreed. Let me take a bath, get dressed. Then we'll spend the day learning about each other's past. But I want to do it downstairs, in the living room. There's a Godzilla movie marathon happening all day today that I've been dying to watch."

Over the next several hours, she learned as much about him as he did about her. How he grew up in Cavendish, spent a few years in the Navy. That he learned that he wasn't nearly as curious about life outside of the small town as he thought he was.

"So," he said, reaching for another handful of popcorn, "I came back. Mom and Dad retired to Florida. He'd never really liked the snow up here in winter. I started doing odd jobs, eventually grew that into being the person to call when water heaters broke or sinks got clogged."

"No big romances, huh?"

He shrugged. "Not really. I mean, I dated. Sure. But never found anyone I wanted to come home to every night. When the people you date and you go back to grade school, it's hard not to remember the days they tried to trip you in the halls. Turned you down for prom."

"I can understand that. Louden's half the size of Cavendish, on a good day when the rodeo's in town. I knew who Bruce was from the first day of school. His family had the money, ran the town. All the girls started fawning over him early on. They wanted the prestige of being on his arm."

"But not you?"

"Nah, not me. I mean, yeah. I was flattered when he asked me to prom. I was the envy of every girl at school. And their target. That's one reason I never reported what he tried to do to me, or the beatings. He was the golden child, could do no wrong. I was the 'lucky' girl that couldn't appreciate what he could do for me. Thing is, I never wanted to be dependent on someone else for any reason. I wanted a life of my own, independent. Not needing a man in my life to pay my mortgage or negotiate my car loan."

"From the sounds of it, that wouldn't have happened in Texas."

"Nope. Bruce had just gotten me fired yet again. He was systematically trying to force me into marrying him by making it impossible for me to support myself." She looked around the house, "When Larry showed up, I leaped at this. It didn't matter what the conditions were in the will. I was promised a place to live about as far away from Bruce as I could get. In two more months, I have legal access to every single dime. I never have to worry about how to pay for anything. The world is mine to explore." Her voice trailed off.

"As long as you're back here for the full moon, though. Right?"

She smiled at him, "Yep. And the job's not hard. Charon's pretty nice. He has a small harp and will play it if there's no souls coming."

The grandfather clock chimed out ten times, startling Amber. "Is it that late already?" She rose and moved aside a curtain. The darkness outside loomed, oppressive and thick. Clouds filled the sky, obscuring the moon.

Heath came up beside her. "That's going to make it harder to know he's coming."

"And come he will." Larry's text alerting her he'd finally gotten to Bangor lit up her phone almost two hours earlier.

She turned. "I want to start getting ready for tonight. Both for what I do outside, and Bruce's arrival. Let's go around the house one more time, make sure everything's locked up. I may not be able to stop him, but I don't have to make it easy for him."

Systematically, she and Heath went through every room in the house plus the basement. Each window was checked to be sure it was locked. Blinds and curtains were shut, making it impossible for anyone outside to see in. Every room, that is, except the mud room.

Heath reached out to drop the blinds while she locked the back door, and she stopped him. "No. Leave those up. I'll be able to unlock the door, but I want you to see Charon if you can. Or have Bruce see me disappear if you can't."

"Think he'll leave if he can't find you out there?"

She shrugged, "No clue. He may see me walk out there and not comprehend a thing that's happening around him. Or he could chase after me and find himself trapped by the snow and river. He will see what Charon allows him to see."

She turned off the light and went into the kitchen. Trying to stay calm, she fed Minerva. There was time yet.

"Heath, I'm going to go up into the attic. I won't be long. You can stay at the base of the ladder if you want to, but you can't go up with me."

"Why not?"

"Amanda created a special room up there. It's a permanent altar, a place for me to find my center. Prepare myself for what may happen tonight. I need to find that calm before he gets here."

"Who? Bruce or Charon?"

She stared at him intently. "Both." Turning, she headed up the stairs to her bedroom.

Entering the closet, she reached behind one of the clothing rods. A thick rope, secured by a hook, came free. Pulling on it, the retractable ladder descended from the ceiling. "You can watch TV in the bedroom, if you want. I shouldn't be more than an hour." She began to climb upward.

Once her head came through the hole in the floor, she stopped. Turning to her right, she found the switch embedded in the floor. Light flooded the space. Climbing in the rest of the way, she worked the rope and pulled the ladder up.

Turning a knob, the roof soundlessly moved aside from the skylights above her. The clouds obscured the sky, but she knew the stars were there. The altar sat in the center of the room. The floor was inlaid with stone to form a pentacle. Wrought iron candleholders sat at each point. Lighting each in turn, she invited the elements to guard her. Only when she felt their presence did she kneel before the altar and begin to meditate.

Time stopped for her when she was in this room usually. But not tonight. It was working against her, and she knew it. She found the peace she needed, the strength to both defend herself and let Bruce be the instrument of his own fate. She clung to the feeling.

Amber was aware that there'd been moments in her life where she was faced with a choice. Take one road or another. It was before her again now. One led her to happiness, a life with Heath, one worth living. The other was being abused, letting those who claimed to love her use her for their own gain.

Drawing a deep breath, she opened her eyes. Whatever would happen in the next hour, she was ready to face it.

She blew out each candle, thanking the elements for their guidance, and covered the skylights. Then, she lowered the ladder and descended back to her room.

Heath wasn't in her room. She glanced at the alarm clock. Two minutes to midnight. Swearing, she dashed to the staircase.

Halfway down, she heard it. The relentless pounding at the front door. She stopped at the landing. Heath stood at the front door, a baseball bat in his hands. Outside, Bruce was shouting, "Gracie! I know you're in there, bitch!" loudly enough that she heard him through the door.

Heath pointed the bat toward the back door. "Go. I'll keep him busy," he told her.

Amber didn't hesitate. She ran down the last few steps and bolted for the fireplace. Her fingers fumbled in haste as she dug to retrieve the bag of coins from their hiding spot. The banging got louder. Bruce's yelling became fiercer, almost primal. Something heavy rammed against the door, echoing down the hallway. She heard the wood begin to crack as Bruce hit it again, trying to break it down.

As soon as she had the bag of coins in hand, she took off for the back door. The transformation had begun already. A loud crash echoed down the hallway. Glancing over her shoulder, she saw Heath back away from what was left of her front door. Bruce's form, heaving, filled the frame. His face, beet red with rage. He saw her. "You're mine, Gracie!" he bellowed.

She saw Heath draw the bat back, ready to swing, and dove for the door. Her hands flew across the locks in a panic, desperate to get outside.

The door finally opened and she rushed down the steps. Her bare feet sank slightly into the warm black sand. Charon stood at the rudder of his boat, one hand removing the hood from his head.

"Who is it, Guardian?" he intoned.

Taking a few deep breaths, Amber found the calm she sought less than ten minutes ago. "One who would harm us both."

"Do your job, Guardian. And I shall do mine if he does not heed you." He reversed his motion, keeping the hood over his head and hiding his face.

She took her place at the halfway point of the dock, waiting. *Please, let no souls come tonight*, she prayed.

The back door swung open, hitting the side of the house with a violent crack. Bruce charged out, dragging someone with him. It was Heath. Or, what was left of him. Amber's heart sank as Bruce tossed Heath's body like a sack of flour. It skidded across the wood, coming to rest not far from her. She grabbed onto the pylon next to her, her fingers willing her to stay put. A small flutter of movement at the base of his throat told her he was still alive. His face was already starting to swell from the beating Bruce had given him.

"See what you did, Gracie? You made me do that to him! If he dies, it's on you! Now, get your ass into my car. We're going home. We're getting married. You are *mine!*" He came within inches of her face. "You're never going to escape me, bitch. I own you," he growled.

Amber met his gaze, and intoned, "Charon comes, to ferry the souls."

Bruce backed away, confusion on his face. "What the hell? Who gives a shit?" He reached out, his hand encircling her forearm and squeezing it painfully.

Wincing in pain, she continued, "Take your seat, he knows where to go."

Her head snapped to one side, the force of the slap making her teeth bite into her cheek. She tasted her own blood. Facing him again, she refused to back down. "The Ferryman knows the sum of your life."

Bruce finally looked past her and saw Charon at the end of the dock. "That one your lover, too? What is it, you get out of Louden and start sleeping around? I always knew you were nothing but a whore!" Violently, he shoved her away.

Her hand grabbed for the pylon to steady herself. She reached into the pouch. She held out her hand, the coins resting in the palm. "Take this coin, pay him when you arrive."

Snorting, Bruce slapped her hand, sending the coins flying. "I'm not paying him for your 'services', slut. I already took care of one of your clients. I can do the same with this one." He leered at her. "And, when I'm done with him, you'd better be ready for me. Because this time you won't get away." He grabbed at her hair, forcing his tongue into her mouth as he kissed her.

She bit down, hard. He yelped. She went flying as he threw her aside. The sand did little to cushion her as she landed. The wind rushed from her lungs. Summoning her strength, she rolled over, expecting him to come after her again.

He stood on the dock, glaring at her. A malicious grin crossed his features. He stooped down, picking up one coin which had landed at his feet. Approaching Charon, he tossed the coin at the Ferryman. "It's more than she's worth, I'm sure," he said as he placed a foot in the craft.

Amber watched in horror, her eyes going wide. Charon caught the coin as it flew his way. His fingers tightened around it, the flesh melting away and leaving bone behind. As Bruce took a seat, Charon turned toward Amber. The handsome features faded as he became the face of Death.

Rising, she slowly made her way over to Heath's prone form as the boat eased away from the shore. The moon came out from behind the clouds, illuminating the scythe that rested on Charon's back.

"Heath, it's going to be okay. Please wake up. I can't carry you back into the house," she whispered, her eyes still focused on the craft as it disappeared in the mist.

Heath's eyes fluttered, opening for a moment. "I can walk, with help. Seeing might be hard until the swelling goes down, though. Where's Bruce?"

A wail of pure terror pierced the silence of the beach. "Bruce is gone," was all she could say.

She helped him get on his feet and they walked back into the house as the snow returned.

Chapter Fifteen
April

"*W*ell, that's it," Larry told her as he put the papers into his briefcase and shut it. The sound of the tumblers on the locks echoing in the courtroom.

"It's over, then?" Amber asked.

"The legal stuff is, yes. You now have full access to all of Amada's estate. Wherever you want to go, whatever you want to do. You fulfilled your six-month obligation. You can leave Cavendish if you want to. No one will stop you."

Amber smiled to herself. She'd stop herself. Trips would be fine, but she knew she'd always be home in time for the full moon.

She rose from the table and followed Larry out of the courtroom. The final legal workings of probate court were now done. No one showed up to contest the will.

They paused outside on the steps of the courthouse. An early warming had melted most of the snow, and Amber found herself admiring the way the trees were showing new growth. "So, what's next for Amber Cross?" Larry asked her.

Squinting at the sun, she smiled. "Time in The Cauldron, for one. Kate and Jessa are finally making the leap. I'm sending them to Scotland for their honeymoon, plus I volunteered to keep the shop open while they're gone."

She felt Larry's hand on her elbow, and she let him guide her down the steps. "What about Louise? Her sentencing is coming up. You can do a victim impact statement to the judge if you want to."

"No, I don't think I need to. She admitted to what she did." She smiled as she saw Heath leaning against her SUV, waiting for her. "She didn't win. Neither did Bruce. I don't think of myself as a victim anyway. I'm a survivor."

Larry stopped, far enough away that Heath couldn't hear him. "I wish we'd found the bear that attacked Bruce. I can't say I was hoping he'd survived the attack, not after what he did to Heath. But the bear could be dangerous to other people."

Amber smiled, "It's okay, Larry. I can promise you that the bear's long gone by now." Leaning over, she kissed him on the cheek. "Thank you. For everything." Skipping down the steps, she joined Heath at the SUV.

His face still bore some bruises from the fight with Bruce, but it was healing. His nose had been broken, and he joked often about how it cured his snoring issues. "Well?" he asked.

"It's all done and official now. You're dating an heiress. How's it feel?"

Heath shrugged, "Dunno. Does that still mean I have to buy you lunch on the waterfront?"

She laughed. "Yeah, you're still on the hook for lunch. And I'm starving!"

Pulling away from him, she ran around to the driver's side and got inside. *Life doesn't get much better than this*, she thought as they pulled away from the curb.

The End

About the Author

Born in the late 60's, KateMarie has lived most of her life in the Pacific NW. While she's always been creative, she didn't turn towards writing until 2008. She found a love for the craft. With the encouragement of her husband and two daughters, she started submitting her work to publishers. When she's not taking care of her family, KateMarie enjoys attending events for the Society for Creative Anachronism. The SCA has allowed her to combine both a creative nature and love of history. She currently resides with her family and two cats in what she likes to refer to as "Seattle Suburbia".

You can find KateMarie at the following sites:

Twitter: @DaughterHauk
FaceBook: http://www.facebook.com/pages/KateMarie-Collins/217255151699492
Her blog: http://www.katemariecollins.wordpress.com

Other Solstice Publishing Titles
By
KateMarie Collins

Daughter of Hauk
Book 1 – The Raven Chronicles

Son of Corse
Book 2 – The Raven Chronicles

Wielder of Tiren
Book 3 – The Raven Chronicles

Mark of the Successor

Arine's Sanctuary

Fin's Magic
A Book of the Amari

Alaric's Bow
A Book of the Amari

A Stab at the Dark

Looking at the Light

Kick the Can

Permafrost

The Rose Box

Challenges Met

28643122R00074

Made in the USA
Columbia, SC
15 October 2018